Something Like
a Storybook

Something Like a Storybook

Sumantra Chattopadhyay

PARTRIDGE

Print information available on the last page.

Author's photograph taken by Anirban Mandal

To order additional copies of this book, contact
Partridge India
000 800 10062 62
orders.india@partridgepublishing.com

www.partridgepublishing.com/india

Contents

To my father Manas Kumar Chattopadhyay

The Condemned

It's raining and raining and it seems that the makers of rain are in no mood to call it a day. As usual we have gathered for inconsequential chatting at our club as we do in the evenings. Most of us are employed in Unemployment Corporation of India and a few have recently lost their 'job' as they have got some ill paid odd job somewhere else. But whatever we do during the day we look forward to this gathering in the evening with the eagerness of people marooned in flood waiting for their daily rations.

Its only quarter to eight but the rain and darkness all around is giving the feeling of late night. In our area heavy rains and power cut go hand in hand. Damn sure that the power lines won't be restored before late afternoon tomorrow. The rains may stop before that but the power supply workers are always punctual. Today we have amidst us a distinguished guest, Basabbabu, who is somewhat distantly related to Tarun, one of our enthusiasts.

It's December, not exactly when rains are expected. But it is raining like any heavy monsoon evening. Our club room, basically made from thatched bamboo, is quite incapable of facing the onslaught of the nature. We are seating on the floor making a close circle with a kerosene lamp at the centre. The diameter of the circle is gradually diminishing as the increased onslaught of the rain is making it impossible to seat near the corners as the windows are failing to hold back the raindrops. We had had two rounds of tea and now seeing the condition I ordered a third round. Fortunately there is a shanty tea shop just next to our club room and Fatik, the owner takes good and bad weathers with stoicism of saints. Amidst all these gloom there is a bright thought of course, after these rains we can expect a really good chill.

- Have you ever attended any hanging?

Chandu suddenly asks Basabbabu. Basabbabu is the jailor of a jail in North Bengal and now is on the verge of retirement. He is a confirmed bachelor and unlike the elderly people, who consider the young folks indecent and unsociable, has got the ability to feel at ease in any sort of company.

- Actually I will be in trouble if you ask me how many hangings I have attended.

Basabbabu answers with a gloomy grin.

- How do they behave when they are taken to the gallows?

Chandu has an insatiable curiosity.

- It is different for different people. Generally they get restless, cry, shout, some turn hostile, but again I have seen cases where the condemned going to the gallows in most decent and cooperative manner possible. One of my uncles was a jailor in the days of the Raj. He used to tell stories of freedom fighters going to gallows in most jovial mood, singing, joking with each other. Unthinkable! I have not been that lucky and such things are not possible without huge inspirations aflame.

- Please share a few experiences.

Now Sunil joins the inquisitive brigade. By this time Fatik has brought tea in earthen cups. We almost pounce on the cups with the eagerness of Shylock looking forward to his 'pound of flesh'. The smokers light cheap cigarettes. Basabbabu doesn't smoke but he doesn't mind either. Our small room becomes full with smoke and the light of the kerosene lamp changes and assumes a mystical nature.

- Do you really think you will enjoy hearing the story of someone being put to death?

But by this time we are all drawn into the snare. After all, animals as we are basically, who doesn't want to hear the story of unnatural death? News of hanging or murder never goes unread. Basabbabu understands he needs to share something to satisfy his junior friends. Rains are still unabated and a light storm is blowing. The darkness, the rains, the sound of the winds which resembled at times the wailing of a distressed and doomed soul made the settings perfect for tales of misery. For a change Basabbabu requested a cigarette, lighted it and started his story.

-     It was a case of murder. Banwarilal, a labour of Lakhotia jute mill had killed his wife with a single blow on the head with a piece of wood used to bolt the door of his hut. It was a common notion that the victim was of questionable character. She used to have male visitors in the evening and Banwarilal always returned late. One day Banwari returned early, unexpectedly of course, and found a man leaving his hut. Prosecution said Banwari killed his wife and left. Just then another woman did come for some errand and found the corpse. People gathered hearing her scream. Banwari was arrested and prosecution attained a quick sentence. Banwari had no means to appoint any pleader and the government prosecutor fighting in his favour was just brilliant. May be without him Banwari had a chance. So condemned Banwari comes to my jail to be hanged.

-     Which jail was it?

Chandu has an eye for the details.

-     Baharampur jail. You people probably know that all jails have special arrangement for condemned prisoners. They are kept in isolation in cells called 'condemned cells'. The first day I went to his cell to meet him I found tears in his eyes. This is very common but somehow, I don't know why, I felt that there is something wrong going on. I went back again after a few days. Saw that he was singing some devotional song looking at the fragment of sky visible from his cell through the small window. He was most well behaved. He sat on the floor and gave me his cot to sit.

Then asked – What date is today, Sir?

I told him the date. He had still fifteen days to breathe the air.

Then asked – Why did you murder your wife Banwari? If she was of questionable nature you could have dumped her. That at least won't lead you to the gallows at the age of twenty eight?

He kept on staring at me for a long time and then said – Can you give me a cigarette Sir?

I used to smoke in those days. It was against the law and I knew that. But could not be rigid with a condemned man and gave him a cigarette and the matchbox. He lit the cigarette slowly, and then said, "I have not murdered my wife Sir. I was returning. I saw a man leave my doors. I entered and found my wife lying dead in a pool of blood. I lost my head and ran out to catch the man. Of course by that time he had vanished."

- But it was proved in court of law that you have committed the crime?

- How can I help that Sir? I have told in the court what had happened. In fact I told that again and again. They didn't accept. I am an illiterate man, what do I know of the circus you call 'law'?

By that time I had read the court conscripts and it was true that Banwari had always pleaded 'not guilty'. "I knew that she is not a good woman" Banwari continued, "But heaven knows I really really loved her. I had tried a lot to reason with her. To make her sober, but I failed. What can a man do in such cases? But, believe me Sir, I have not killed her."

One question was peeping in my mind for some time and now I let it out.

- Why did she behave like that Banwari?

- She was addicted to gold Sir. She used her vicious earnings to make ornaments. I could provide her bread but not gold. And ultimately that gold took her life and now I you are going to kill me...

- Gold took her life!

- She was wearing a gold necklace when I left for work...it was not there on her corpse.

I left him for that day. After that I have visited him several times. We had talks. Always gave him a cigarette. He used to talk of his four year old daughter. He was worried of her future. I had little to say. We both knew what fate loomed for her in all probability. The libido of the city and so called civilization would one day welcome her through the gates of the Hades.

But just two days before the hanging his attitude changed completely. I got the report that Banwari is making a huge fuss. I went to his cell. He was shouting.

-    Is it some kind of weird joke? I am innocent and you will hang me!

I told him, "Control yourself Banwari. What's the use? You have only a day in between and then you have to go. And none of us can do anything about it. Rather think of God. I will send you some devotional songs"

The stout young man broke down in tears.

-    Save me Sir, I am innocent, believe me, I am innocent.

There was nothing else I could do so I came back. Called the jail doctor and asked him to have a look at Banwari and give him some sedation if necessary.

* * *

Then came the day of hanging and as I was getting ready at the dead of night the phone rang. It was a call from Kolkata. The hanging stood cancelled! The actual murderer had been nabbed for another crime. When put to police beatings he had admitted that he had killed Moti, Banwari's wife, for the necklace. I immediately called up the assistant jailor, and asked him to inform Banwari. He was then being prepared for hanging. And that's what I shouldn't have….

-      So after all he was not hanged?

Chandu was clearly unhappy as he was looking for stories of hanging after all just like the rest. Basabbabu remained silent for some time and then looked up with a strange look.

-      No, he was spared. I went to his cell. He was shouting, crying, "I am saved hahaha I am saved So you could not hang me after all, hahahahaah"

He was stark naked and completely mad!

It was fourteen years ago. Till date Banwari is a permanent inmate of a lunatic asylum. Once I had visited him. He has to be kept in chains. And whenever he is awake he either shouts or pinches himself to verify that he is 'alive'.

*   *   *

The rain is yet to stop. But we leave the room and ignoring the downpour practically flee to our respective homes. We are feeling scared. We are chilled to the bones but that is not only for the rain.

We all can hear, "I am saved hahaha I am saved; so you could not hang me after all, hahahahaah"

Libido

The coffee is getting cold and after a few minutes even highest level of generosity won't prevent describing the coffee as undrinkable. Rupa has gone back to the kitchen. Indra toyed with the idea of leaving silently but then dropped it. It would be closer to truth to say that he is not in a position to leave because he is stuck, just as flies get stuck in marmalade on slices of left over after breakfast. And just like the fly he is thinking of ways to escape because he is damn confident that the company of Rupa and the conversations to follow will be as stale and detestable as the coffee, What makes the situation more bitter is the thought that Indra has meticulously planned the meeting and had drawn a rosy picture of the events, he thought, would follow naturally.

Indra is a junior executive of a new generation engineering company. He has passed from a private engineering college just a few months back and unlike most of his peers he has been able to bag a job quite fast thanks to his looks and smartness. Only yesterday he got the news that their senior director Parekh is on ventilation and the chances of revival are next to nothing. Parekh had had pacemaker installed. But he openly flouted all rules to be followed by a man of his age and physical conditions. He used to drink like a fish and red meat was his staple diet. So what has happened can be described as 'historical inevitability', thought Indra.

He had learnt the term when he was aligned with Left politics for some time while he was in first year. His interest was not in politics but some good looking young ladies who used to visit the union room and as he had not much luck with them his interest in politics dropped too.

Today he got the news that Parekh has passed away last night and office will be closed after first half in his honour. Anticipating this Indra had checked and found that Rupa would be at home the whole day.Indra had not put the question tacitly enough Rupa was a bit surprised. Why is Indra interested in her whereabouts when he would be slogging at the computer as part of daily paid detention programme pompously called 'job'.

Generally Indra keeps his daily smoking limited to five cigarettes but today he bought a full pack of ten and then took two bears from the liquor shop. This is the first time he has stepped in the liquor shop without friends accompanying him. He had to check the surroundings several times before stepping in. But today things are different, for the first time in life he is going to meet Rupa with no one else present around. Rupa's parents are in office at this hour and Rupa is enjoying vacation after her BA exams. Indra realized that he is excited and is sweating even in this December day.

He has got certain plans but not sure about success because Rupa is quite highly opinionated woman and, secretly though, Indra is afraid of her mood swings. Human trainsof thought follow strange trajectories. Thinking of Rupa's mood within seconds Indra thinks of 'Moods' and stops in front of a pharmacist. Cautious as Rupa is she may demand Indra to be ready with the necessary precaution. But buying a pack of condoms is not easy particularly given the circumstances.

Indra spots a cigarette and soft drink shop opposite to the pharmacist and goes there. He takes two small bottles of coke and smokes a cigarette to boost his confidence. Amassing all the smartness at his disposal he walks to the counter and demands a pack of Moods. (Basically he was imitating the gait of the gentleman who features in a condom ad in a TV commercial). The middle aged gentleman at the counter has noticed that while smoking on the other side of the road Indra was eyeing his shop with the looks of a shoplifter planning a pick and run. The facts that Indra almost tripped at the door of the shop and is constantly licking his lips as they are running dry didn't help much to conceal the hurricane he is experiencing within. The gentleman cannot not help making a little fun of Indra's 'fish out of water' state and says, 'what would you prefer Sir, normal or ribbed?'

'Normal' Indra is almost inaudible.

The man pulls out a big plastic bag. And then displaying a gallery of stained teeth asks, "Trust you have change, I just gave all I had to the last customer"

Indra feels at lurch. He has never purchased a pack of condoms before so whether it costs ten or hundred he was totally unaware of. Without letting the conversation roll further he hands out a hundred rupee note. He takes the pack comes to the road and heaves a sigh of relief and proceeds towards Rupa's home.

Rupa is surprised to find Indra as the visitor. Not that he is most welcome as she is alone at home and she knows pretty well that desire may raise its head finding Rupa alone in a vacant apartment. Rupa is in a negligee without any inners as she was having a nap and the only visitor expected at this hour is the old maid. Anyway after all she cannot turn him away from the door so ushers him in and goes inside to cover her in a dressing robe.

- You at this hour! Have bunked office?
- Not exactly. Actually one of the directors has passed away so we had a condolence meeting and it was called a day. Thought of meeting you…seems I have disturbed your nap
- Its okay…like some coffee?
- No…no coffee…chilled bear…I have the stock

Indra lightly pulls Rupa's hand and makes her sit next to him. The uneasiness that Rupa had felt seeing Indra at the door is now shooting up. She is not totally unaccustomed to drinking bear, but doing so at home is a strict no no.

- Keep the bear for your home and friends and let me get us some coffee.
- I cannot…I have got no privacy and bear is treated as alcohol with lots of taboo
- Same is the case here…so better find some joint and enjoy it with your friends.

Some 'experienced' friends of Indra have advised that one should not jump into the 'act'…the trick is creating the right mood.The rebuff on the bear issue has dampened the mood, but it's no time to show disgust, it's time for patience.

-    What's the big hurry…coffee can wait…rather turn on the TV

Rupa turns on the TV and sits beside Indra and together they watch a cricket match for some time. Indra smokes a cigarette and then suddenly putting his arm on Rupa's shoulder draws her close. Rupa knew all the while this is coming and does not protest. She knows that she has to play safe and try not to hurt Indra's feelings. Her affair with Indra is an open secret at home, mother has clear support and father has no loud objection. That her father has no objection to the relationship is of course easily construable from her mother's support. Rupa has never, since her childhood, seen her mother to voice opinion that is contrary to the opinion of her father. With time many changes have comein this house. The plasma TV has replaced the old big TV set with picture tube; the old rattling scooter has given way to a neat hatch back car. But mother's position has remained unaltered.

Now though her mom has accepted Indra as her prospective son in law she has laid down certain 'commandments' for Rupa. Indra's presence at this hour is not at all conducive for following those dictates. Rupa allows Indra up to an extent but the big point is will Indra stop there? Already Indra's hand has entered Rupa's blouse and freely moving around, pressing, pinching. Rupa has lightly voiced her protest several times but today Indra is unstoppable. Indra's hand has started its journey sliding down Rupa's belly. When Indra tries to tug at the elastic of her panty Rupa stops him. Enough is just enough!

- But why Rupa, we are going to get married anyway?
- That's fine...then wait till that happens
- What's the harm in starting now? Its natural... everybody does it...and I have come prepared.
- I am sorry Indra...I have some values which I cannot shrug off just like that.
- Damn it! These sentiments are baseless...
- They are not baseless to me at that's final.

Rupa gets up and leaves. She returns with the tray with coffee mugs and sits at a distance. Suddenly it has dawned upon her that the maid is on leave today. Some political party has called a rally and as always she has to attend it mandatorily. So it boils down to the fact that Rupa has to ward Indra till her mom returns from work. Indra on the other hand is feeling that he bumping his head again and again against a stone wall. He is bleeding profusely but there not a scratch on the wall. He decides to leave.

A few days ago he has experienced a strange dream. It seemed that he is with Rupa standing on a shore. There is a small hill on one side of the shore blocking off the view after a turn. He is stark naked and Rupa is properly dressed as expected. The shore is deserted except these two souls. Indra is insisting Rupa to strip to which Rupa is not consenting. At one point he loses patience and tries to strip Rupa forcefully. Rupa somehow manages to break free and runs with Indra running behind her. Rupa vanishes at the turn and when Indra reaches there he find Rupa nowhere. But this place is not deserted. Some fishermen and women are looking at naked Indra quite agape. Indra is dying to find a place to hide.

Many a times Indra has tried to imagine Rupa without clothes. Since his imagination is not that prolific he has not been exactly successful and so he has taken the easy way out. He regularly scans the pornographic sites and spotting a photo of a completely naked woman having slight resemblance with Rupa he has saved the photo with the name 'Rupa nude.jpg'. He uses the photo when he is too excited. Today is not the first episode of failure but today's refusal is unbearable. While walking to bus stop Indra decides that he will delete that photo from his computer and has to give a serious thought whether or not to continue the relationship. He has to do something else as well, so he calls his friend Jishnu.

*   *   *

The dies is cast, Jishnu was of great help. The guy is a real 'go-getter'. After toying with the idea for a night Indra had called the number supplied by Jishnu and struck the deal. It belongs to one escort service provider code named as Rex. Rex did send him the photos of the girls immediately and very quickly Indra had replied back with his choice. This time he ensured that the girl doesn't resemble Rupa in any way. In past two days he has developed a strong detest not only for Rupa but also for any woman who even remotely resembles Rupa. Rex replied that the lady is available on such and such date but her rate is high. She is an air hostess who flies in and out of the city and utilizes the time in between. Indra was ready to pay the price and the timings were fixed.

Indra has reached the venue which is a hotel in EM Bypass. Rex has arranged it all as part of the package. Jishnu, much experienced as he is, has given some valuable tips. The payment must be made upfront. Indra should not hurry. A chilled beer and light music helps in getting into the mood. It's better not to shy away and clearly inform the lady that it his first experience. They take special care for 'first timers'. Indra finds everything in order; he has to wait for about half an hour and lights a cigarette tries to relax.

After that afternoons' refusal Indra had met Rupa once in a restaurant. Indra was unthinkably bitter and rude. Among hordes of other banter Indra has expressed that in her dress and ways of life Rupa is after all a highly backdated girl. Rupa had only responded with silence. At times she was wiping off tears from the corner of her hankie with passion flowers embroidered in it. Her tears gave Indra sort of perverse pleasure. He is feeling the same pleasure in waiting for Selina now. The manager has called once in the intercom to ask whether Indra needs anything. These hotels are practically make-shift brothels and run on 'hourly-basis'. It takes the hotel stuff just a few seconds to understand who are regular visitors and for whom it is the debut. The debutants can be 'milked' freely as nervous as they are and afraid of law they say 'no' to nothing. Indra wonders why Selina is late. Jishnu has said that these women are very professional and punctuality is there trade mark. Indra calls Rex but finds the number busy.

The bell rings. By now Indra has almost finished half the bottle of bear. Indra feels a bit nervous but quickly pulls him together, gets up, tidies his hair and opens the door. He is greeted with a light cloud of smoke; Selina is smoking some cheap cigarette with a strange smell. As the smoke clears a bit Indra spots a mole on the right shoulder of Selina just like on Rupa's shoulder. Indra leaves the door to make way for Selina and settles back in the chair. She enters the room with dignified gait, looks around and settles herself in a couch. She then takes the remote control and turns down the temperature setting of the air conditioner. Indra is perspiring profusely. In the past he has never seen Rupa in such lascivious dress. He picks up the glass of beer tries to gulp it down and breaks up in a bout of cough.

When the cough subsides Rupa says, "Can I have a beer please?'

Indra finds his hand shaking while pouring the beer. The shake of his hand is joined by the vibration of his cell phone. It is Rex calling.

Before Indra could burst out in anger Rex said in his artificial friendly manner, 'Sorry man Selina could not make it…as her flight got awfully delayed so I have sent Romi. Let me tell you her customer rating is sky high. Bye, enjoy yourself.'

Silence is not always silent as chill is not exactly cold at times. Right now there is no noise in the room except the light buzz of the air conditioner. But Indra is feeling loud clatter within his head and trying in vain to shut off the same and remain calm. The air conditioner shows twenty three degree Celsius but he feels he is out in a hot desert at midday. Rupa is slowly sipping at her beer and smoking a cigarette. So this is of the how Rupa maintains her luxurious lifestyle? And this is the woman he was going to marry? Now how can they face each other as he knows her profession and she has found out to what depths his libido can drive him?

Rupa is through with the bear. She wipes her lips with the same embroidered handkerchief and says in most matter of fact tone, "I don't think you can make any use of my presence. I need the payment anyway. I have to share a percentage with Rex plus there are costs for all these". Rupa shows the room. "And by the way a few of your books are lying in my place, I will leave them with my mom. Collect them at your convenience."

*   *   *

Rupa has left with the payment. Indra tips the waiter and comes out. Now he feels a bit steady. The waiter hails a cab for him. Indra knows what he has to do first thing when he reaches home. He has to read a particular page of Sydney Sheldon's "If Tomorrow Comes". It contains a quite graphic portrayal of love making. Jishnu is bound to call and nothing short of a detailed description will satisfy him.

The Game Plan

As a rule we respect the qualities of our enemies much more than we do so of our friends. The virtues of his wife Soma that Partha not only remembers but reveres too are punctuality and fixity of purpose. Once her mind is made up she will do it and there is nobody or nothing that can budge her. This steadfastness has at times been cause of her husband's displeasure and Partha is not that sort who gulps down displeasures silently, but those had little effect on Soma. But today to his utmost surprise and angst Soma is not behaving her normal self. The clock is ticking on and a little more delay will foil all efforts. Partha thinks of calling the man but then remembers it's of no use as now he will receive no call.

Partha Mukherjee is one of the leading hoteliers of the city. He fully owns four hotels in various parts of the city and is the owner of big shares in many others. Apart from these he has invested in various types of businesses. He is the owner of a bungalow in New Alipore, a fleet of cars, enjoys membership of three most costly clubs, i.e. he possess everything necessary to brand a man 'highly successful' in this consumerist world. His only son Sambit is settled in States where the couple pays a visit once a year. Sambit is too busy to save his job and cannot manage to visit his native land. But that is no issue in Partha's life, the crisis is elsewhere.

Partha cannot remember last when he had some sweetness left in his marriage but now he has practically reached the edge of the precipice. When he got married some thirty years back Partha was partner and manager in a small hotel. Soma also hails from a very ordinary background. Her father, a lower division clerk in a government department was sort of relieved to get her daughter married off without getting all his resources depleted. Three years after the marriage Partha managed to buy out the other partners and became the owner of the hotel. And the wheel started rolling since then. His friends say that his wife is his lady luck and are openly envious from the belief.While Partha admits the value of the support he had received from Soma he knows for sure that only luck has not got him where he is now. The tips of a trident that has made the progress possible are strong business acumen, indefatigable nature and readiness todo anything in the interest of business. This last attribute of nature is causing all trouble.

The trouble started some one year back when, purely by chance, Soma came to know of one of Partha's misdeeds committed fifteen years earlier. At that point of time Partha owned two medium sized hotels. A multinational hotelier running two hotels in Kolkata was planning to acquire more hotels. Partha was approached with the request of selling his two hotels to this brand. As one of the then ministers were behind the project the request was actually more of a threat. Some other hoteliers of Kolkata were under the same threat when one incident changed the scenario rather dramatically. The only daughter of sister in law of the minister was kidnapped and her body was found after three days in a room of one of the two hotels owned by the MNC brand. Though theculprit remained anonymous like Jack the Ripper it was disclosed that the lady used to frequent the hotel and spend the nights here with her male friend or friends.

Not only did this incident frustrate the expansionist ambitions of the MNC, they had to sell off their business within a year and leave. Suddenly, due to carelessness of Partha Soma did come to know of Partha's involvement in this ghastly incident. Though Partha tried to make her understand that the murder was not part of the plan and it was rather an accident, Soma is far from convinced. Things started going wrong with Soma since then and now Soma is almost putting up threats that she will disclose everything to the police. She is in possession of some evidence which will enable the police to reconstruct the case and destroy Partha.

So Partha has hit upon a simple but very effective game plan. Sambhu and Aslam are waiting with two big loaded trucks at a particular street corner seldom manned by the traffic guards. Their instructions are simple and precise; they have to crush the small hatch back of Soma when it arrives. All these wouldn't have been necessary if Soma were a bit less moralistic and more practical. Soma would not see the fact that without that 'mishap' there was no way the MNC could be stopped. With their financial strength and political clout they would have made Partha sell off his business at throwaway price. Soma also vehemently opposes the practice of regularly bribing various government and bank officials as she fails to understand that these are mere 'rules of the game' and were set long before Partha's grandfather was born.

Partha's steady girlfriend Ananya Biswas is good looking, smart suave and has got the same predatory instincts as possessed by Partha. She holds a prominent post in Partha's group of hotels and inevitably accompanies Partha in all his tours. Partha believes that for a man of his class this is only natural and wives of such people should be turning a blind eye to these matters. But Soma, true to her middle class background, cannot digest Partha's escapades. Though minor, this is one of the reasons, of drawing up today's game plan.

Partha knew that Soma would leave precisely at five thirty PM and go to Academy of Fine Arts to visit the exhibition of paintings of her friend Soham. Even yesterday he heard Soma talking with Soham confirming her attendance. Soma drives her own car. Partha has also checked the Times for the notification of the exhibition. Today is the perfect day for such operations because the streets would be nearly deserted. A day and night cricket match is going on between India and Pakistan and the gentry of the city are glued to the television sets since afternoon. But the problem is Soma seems to be totally relaxed and in no mood to go out.

After some time Partha can't help it any more.

- Won't you go to the exhibition?
- I think I should not...not feeling well

- What happened?
- Nothing in particular...just...
- For that you will miss your friend's first big exhibition?
- Will go there tomorrow
- You have invited the Mehta family tomorrow
- They are coming for lunch...I will go at six
- Lunch! They are coming at five in the evening.
- What? They have changed the time and you didn't even inform me!
- Sorry...just missed it
- Ok...anyway will attend some other exhibition of Soham, it's not the last one

Light beads of perspiration appear in Partha's brow. Fifty percent advance payment has been made. The crooks as they are most likely they are going to charge extra for the time lost.

- But I am surprised to see you breaking your head over art exhibitions?

Partha senses alarm. She is right. He has never expressed interest in art and has always talked of art and artists in extreme negative. And at that moment the idea dawns on him.

- Well...today Bikash Bhattacharya is coming to the exhibition...
- Oh really! But Soham didn't say so
- Even Soham doesn't know, this is a surprise gift for his favourite student

- But how could you know?
- From the president of the Gallery is my client...I manage all their events.

Soma is a connoisseur of art and almost worships the famous painter Bhattacharya. Partha knew all these. His ploy comes in handy. But still there is some questions he has to face.

- But still...why are you so insisting...you care a fig about art. It would have been natural to think that you are going to bring some woman in so you want the coast to be clear...but that's also rules out...I know you very well...you leave yourphilandering out of the premises of the house...so what can be the reason?
- Why don't you think that nowadays I am taking some interest in art...man changes with time
- Not exactly convincing...but I will think of it later... now let me get ready.

She gets ready in no time and leaves in her car. Partha gives a wry smile thinking of Soma's statement claiming that she knows him. Partha believes that it's practically impossible for anyone to know someone else who is alive. The reason is simple. There is nothing more transient in the world than the psyche of a man. It is always changing.

Partha gives a ring to Aslam exactly five minutes after Soma's departure. Aslam disconnects the call as planned. It is one of the maladies of modern civilization that more effective communications are made through missed calls than calls that are received, thinks Partha.

He settles in his favourite couch with scotch. Soma will need fifteen minutes to reach the spot where the trucks are waiting, i.e. ten minutes from now there will be the crash. So in likelihood the 'information' of the crash and fatality will come after about forty minutes. Partha heaves a sigh of relief...no more tension, no more fearing his alter ego, no more hindrance in making merry with Ananya. Partha has complete confidence in Aslam. It's not the first time Partha is taking his services. Years back an overenthusiastic reporter had managed to gather some information that one of his small hotels was used regularly for shooting of X-rated films. He was offered a price but he refused to be purchased. His scooter and his corpse were found in a canal beside the bypass both in equally sorry state and almost beyond recognition. But Partha is not inhuman, his wife now sings in one of the bars secretly owned by him. He himself of course remained anonymous all the while. People should be aware of the lengths of their leap; Partha had thought sadly when he heard that Aslam had accomplished his job of crushing the reporter.

Since year before last doctor has put a strict ban on his smoking and Partha obeys the doctor. But today everything is different. In fact he has smoked two cigarettes already today. Soma must have smelled the tobacco but didn't comment. She doesn't bother herself on such matters these days.

Partha lights a cigarette and suddenly, out of nowhere in fact, remembers that night when he fainted while laughing heartily. The matter could have been quite fateful as Partha was driving when it happened. It was their first long drive in the new car. Later on Partha came to know that Soma somehow stopped the car jamming on the break from the side seat. Then he shifted Partha to her seat and somehow managed to drive five miles before she could find a doctor. Novice as she was driving long five miles in dusty bumpy dark village road with her husband panting for breath was no easy task. But why is Partha reflecting on those days now? That relationship is over years back and in a few minutes the phone will ring to inform that she is no more.

But today the theme of death is looming so large that Partha is constantly reminded of episodes of deaths just like some unending television series which are repulsive yet riveting. Partha did lose his eight year old son, Sagnik. Sagnik left after suffering a fever just for five days. He was too shattered to go back to work and drowned his days and nights in alcohol. Soma gulped down her own sense of loss and did pull up Partha from that abyss. Many of his well-wishers were constantly advising him to sell of all business establishments. Had it not been for the support of his wife, who was also equally shattered by her son's death but didn't show, Partha would have sold off everything in throwaway price and the well-wishers would have booked penthouses with their commissions from the buyers.

Then with time Partha's business has come uphill his conjugal life has gone downhill almost in equal pace. Partha doesn't know if there is any relation between these two journeys but honestly these matter little now when he has already put her head in the guillotine.

A little later the call will come and he will have to rush to the spot. He will have to identify the corpse. In all likelihood the corpse will be beyond recognition. This reminds Partha of a past incident and he instantly feels heavily nauseated. Partha's father was killed in a train accident that happened in a place called Gaishal. The mortuary attendant had opened the drawer with a sinister rumbling noise and Partha had to look at the corpse of his father. Though the semi mutilated and crushed body was almost beyond recognition Partha could recognize instantly. He didn't feel any pain, sense of loss or anything of that kind though, neither it was possible to recap the hardships this man had undertaken to bring him up. The sight of the trampled corpse coupled with most unsavoury smell made Partha run out of the dreary room and he started vomiting. Soma did take all the trouble of finishing the formalities, dealt with the undertakers and had arranged the cremation. Partha only managed to go to the crematorium just before putting the corpse in the furnace. Who is going to do all those things now? He cannot wait for his son to arrive from States. And so now he will be alone and the helping hand that was always there in moments of crisis won't be there.

Partha suddenly realizes that he is not feeling well. "What the hell is happening to me!" thinks Partha, "this is not the time for being emotional. Rather I will have to be steady, very steady." Actually the demand of the hour is much more that being only steady. It requires display of acting skills. He has to show astonishment, grief, despair and at the same time everything must be heavily controlled.

Over and above all these he must be very careful about talking to the police and the press. In fact he has silently rehearsed the lines he will say to both these quite a few times. The entertainment page of the English daily is lying in front of him and it has a big cover story on a stage actor who has been recently awarded the life time achievement award for his contribution to theatre. But the real achievements in life go unsung most of the time thinks Partha. Nobody would ever recognize his talent of acting, for example when he would perform the last rites, or talk to the press or attend the meeting organised by the chamber of commerce to pay homage to the memories of Soma.

An electronic sound starts. Partha first looks at his cell phone; it's not a call. And then he understood it is the sound of a reminder coming from the clock radio. It's medicine time for Partha who has to take some medicines that regulates his systolic and diastolic pressures. He is quite forgetful of this evening dose so Soma has set this alarm. Though their relation is next to nothing Soma never forgets such chores. In his childhood Partha had witnessed tumultuous days in Kolkata as a radical Leftist movement was going. Since then he is accustomed to the sound of bombs. But he had no clue that the electronic chirp of the imported and highly sophisticated radio clock can sound like a bomb too. The chirp created sort of Tsunami in Partha.

What is it he is doing! He is no less responsible for the sorry state of his conjugal life. Not only has he forgotten the fact that a relationship is an endless creative pursuit, he has in fact, in many an occasion, been a vandal in destroying it. And today he is going to kill her for that!

Partha, unknown to himself, lets out an animal like cry, and runs to fetch his car key. The servants have been granted a day off so there was none to lock the door. Neither does he care now. Partha drove out of the apartment at high speed in his BMW startling the men in charge of apartment security. The machine roared through the empty roads of Kolkata just like an animal jerked out untimely of its peaceful slumber. It's no use calling Aslam now. Even driving at this speed may not save the situation. But Partha has to try.

As the roads are nearly vacant and he is driving oblivious to the traffic signals he very soon reached the spot where the accident is to be staged. It is planned that it will occur on a flyover. When Partha is at the point of ascent to the flyover he spots the Soma's car and Aslam's truck. The truck is following the car from a safe distance. Partha knows at a particular point the truck will suddenly gain speed and will hit the small hatchback at a particular angle with unfailing precision and the car will be tossed off the bridge and it will fall on the rail tracks some fifty feet below. Aslam will vanish with his truck. Soma and Aslam are very close to the spot and Aslam is changing direction. The only way to stop him is to speed up and get his BMW between Aslam's truck and Soma's car. That way Aslam will have to drop or at least alter his plan. Partha steps on the gas. But as speed of no machine created on earth match the speed of mind his plan does not work out to the ultimate detail. By the time Partha manages to position his car behind Soma's car

Aslam has already gained the killing speed and there is no holding back. Aslam's car rams heavily at the BMW. The car knocks off part of the railing and almost by sheer magic the car stops at the edge with front left wheel hanging in thin air. Aslam utters a filthy accusation and leaves with his truck. Hearing the noise of the car Soma has parked at a side. Now she embarks and comes near the now broken BMW and immediately recognizes the car and the man in the driver's seat. She lets out a scream and runs to Partha who is unconscious and profusely bleeding.

Going by medical logic Partha should have been sitting on the clouds the moment he was hit by the truck. But at times God feels moody and loves to indulge in His whims so when Partha is taken to ICU he is still alive. To the extreme astonishment of the medical brigade Partha lives through the crisis, though he is rendered paralytic with the lower portion of his body totally non-functional. The sense of loss that Partha felt was considerably lessened by a feeling of relief on knowing that he has been able to save the life of Soma.

Partha now moves around in a wheel chair. He goes to office does his usual chores and comes back. Police have failed to catch hold of the killer truck. His office work is now considerably light as Partha has sold off his big hotels. Ironically most of them have been bought by the same MNC. One day Partha didn't think twice to stoop to hell to stop this MNC from entering the Kolkata market. Times have changed and so is the case with the person. From an aggressive hotelier with strong predatory instincts today Partha is a person who is sober at heart and sober in disposition. But these changes are dwarfed by another change that has occurred rather silently. Today Soma and Partha have come close to each other. Partha is discovering Soma every day and thoroughly enjoying the process.

Marriage in general is characterized by a particular kind of selfish love and desire for erotic dominations. For the first time in life Partha is enjoying the company of Soma free from these common attributes. Partha can realize though that he is severely lacking the force of life and the little that he has left can come to an end any day.

The fairy tales normally end with the line "And they lived happily ever after". In actuality however nothing that does not end ceases to be sweet after certain time. If man were immortal no man woman relationship would have lasted in the world. In this case the nearness to the end is making the time so valuable, even the everyday talk so sweet.

They never talked of death but intelligent as she is Soma can also feel that the curtain may drop any time and without much of a warning. The process of discovering the other person is happening both ways. Soma today feels that she could have shown bit more patience and compassion. Instead her bitter criticism has always pushed Partha more and more to the very acts she criticized.

In a summer day, without any warning the sky is suddenly overcast with clouds and in no time a severe Norwestar lashes on the city. Traffic comes to a dead stop as many of the trees in Southern Avenue fell with frightening noise.

Suddenly Partha feels just like that the trees didn't know that their ends are so near his end may be waiting just round the corner!

What if he gets no chance to talk?
What if there is no tomorrow for him?

He suddenly becomes restless and implores Soma to come and sit near him. He has got something to say and that cannot wait. Soma loves the rains and she was merrily busy in the kitchen. But Partha won't listen to anything, he has to talk and he has to talk now. Soma gives in to this childish headstrong attitude and comes to hear what has become so importantsuddenly.

For a long time Partha could not stare at Soma.

Then slowly he began.

"That night I did plan to get you killed. It was no accident. The truck was paid to crush your car. I know...after hearing this you may not like me to stay here...I don't mind...I will go away in the morning...but I had to tell you...my days are numbered...I can feel it...you can hate me...I deserve it... and one more thing...you can share the fact with our son. I deserve his scorn too...but I had to tell. Even if that means I die alone in some loveless sanatorium."

Soma asks, "Why didn't you kill me then? You had an impeccable plan."

It's impossible for him to put into words the answer for this "Why?" Partha only nods his head and said "I couldn't. And honestly I am glad because I couldn't"

Soma draws her seat closer to Partha and says, "Then I should also share with you the fact that I know what you just said. In fact I knew it even before the day I was supposed to be killed. Actually Aslam's wife somehow came to know of the game plan. She was a regular in the NGO I run. She had spilled the beans to me"

The astonishment is so great that it takes Partha some time and considerable effort to talk.

"But then why the hell did you go out that night?" he ultimately blurted out.

Soma draws deep breath and says, "I was overcome by deep sense of hurt. At first I was agitated, I thought of running to the police and put you behind bars. But then just as evening comes slowly and then moves into night, my mind got filled with deep darkness. I thought if my husband, with whom i have spent the longest part of my life and have faced so many storms together, can decide to kill me, then so be it. I asked the meaning of life. I asked do I deserve to live after such a big failure."

"Failure!" Partha still cannot understand what to say.
"Of course it is a gigantic failure. A life is meaningless without a relation and this relation is meaningless as it is making someone plan to kill me. So I felt I do not deserve to live. I have seen life and why should I greedily cling to

it when I am not wanted? So I left with my car that day with due mental preparation, didn't know that I will have to return."

The storm has subsided but still the wind is blowing strong. The streets are dark as the falling trees have broken the power supply cables. So is the room. Only a battery lamp kept on a side table is giving little light making movement possible. Partha and Soma remain seated side by side for a long time.

Then Partha asks, "But then why did you stay with me. Why did you make it a mission to get me recovered?"

Soma leans towards Partha, gives a sweet smile, shuffles his hair and says, "The fault is all yours. You didn't let me die after all!"

Death of a Cynic

I have breathed my last a little while ago in the ICU of a famous hospital. This hospital is so costly that people who get admitted here, or their near and dear ones, make it a point to publicise that they can afford to get treated here. Quite naturally my wife did the same when I was admitted some ten days back.

As yet she is unaware of the fact that I am no more. How would she know? The people who are paid to declare the deaths don't know it either. These clowns have installed lot of gadgets around me and one of those confounded things is pumping air into my lungs and drawing it out with pre-set regularity. So my chest is heaving up and down. It can be said with the help of modern engineering a dead man is performing perfectly in the role of a man who is 'alive'.

It all started last to last Friday. It was a usual working day. Did attend the board meeting where as usual I maligned others for something which was actually my fault, ensured that number of people are laid off blaming it on 'hard recession hit' times. Also did lovingly pat and squeeze the arse of my new secretary who is quite a damsel to make her understand what is expected from her when she will be accompanied me in the ensuing business trip to Delhi.

Also had had my share of drinking and flirting in the club where I go three days in a week. Then returned home and started 'work' in my study with two pegs of good scotch. My computer monitor is very strategically placed so that only I can see it. I watch quality porn keeping a few work related files open. Remaining prepared for unwelcome challenges is an important corporate lesson that has become an instinct now. My friend Prabir is a greater connoisseur of quality erotica and he has so kindly driven me to these exciting web addresses. Scotch with erotica form a lovely duo.

As usual even on that day I was enjoying Scotch with Debjani. Debjani is the name of my new personal secretary and I love to use it as a personal code for the exposed women in the porn. I knew after the Delhi trip I would have another folder with nude photos of Debjani. I have a collection of nude photos of all women I have slept with. They bring back sweet memories and also prove to be handy if these women try to act smart.

Suddenly I felt an eerie sensation and little uneasiness. After so much of fried food at the club a bout of acidity was only normal and was just thinking of taking an antacid when suddenly I felt a sharp excruciating pain as if someone is holding my heart in a vice and then everything blacked out. I fell with my chair making a loud crash. I knew that was the end and at the last moment of consciousness a face did flash in my mind. I couldn't recognize it was not Jhimli, my wife, nor my son or daughter or my parents. The face came as a flash and then it was darkness like I had never seen before.

I have just regained consciousnesses a little while ago. I found I am somewhere I don't know or never had been before. It was a shabby room, smelly and ill ventilated, sort of the type I make my servants live and pay them less as they are offered living quarters. And to add to my dismay a man was standing in front of me, equally shabby and ill dressed.

I told him, "Who are you? You look like the un-loaders who work in my factory sheds. How could you make entry into my house?"

The man smiled.

"Un-loader is a good term for me" he said, "That's exactly what I have been doing since time immemorial"

"So this man wants to win me with jugglery of words" I thought. "He has no idea what a tough nut I am"

So I said," Look here man, if you are expecting alms or donations of any kind make good through the door. I only pay donations to ladies' club and that too not unconditionally"

The man smiled again. There was a strange quality in the smile. Anyone would think that the man being unsure whether it was fit to smile or cry has chosen a gesture that can be interpreted either way.

He said, "No Sir, it is not your house and I have gone nowhere. Actually you have come to visit me. Now look" Saying this he turned round and pressed a button and just as it happens in theatres a wall receded with a mechanical buzz. And then I saw this ICU, worried people all around including my wife Jhimli and 'me' lying in the bed with oxygen musk and n number of tubes inserted into my body. It took a little time to recognize myself. After all who in the world has got this opportunity to look at his own self except in a mirror? Right at this moment a man with a lot of authority entered the scene with some subordinates following.

I had had my education in a suburban school run by the Christian missionaries and they used to distribute copies of the Holy Bible with pictures. Always there was a picture of Jesus with a yellow ring behind His head. Once I did innocently ask the Father why has that man a yellow light behind his head? Father explained that it is called 'halo' and is there with all divine entities.

My friend Babin was an imp of the first order. He made a 'halo' with thermocol and lit it with some cells and small bulbs and came to the class and declared "See I am now a divine entity"! The thing got reported to the Head Master and Babin was caned. I had a question in my mind? If the divine entities have got a halo of light then does the representatives of the Hades have concentrated darkness behind their heads? But as I didn't want myself to be exposed to the risk of being caned I preferred to leave my question unuttered.

Now I can see many a thing hitherto invisible to me. Like I can see that everybody around have got more or less dark patches behind their heads but the authoritative man who just entered is like carrying a big black hole behind his head. I immediately understood that this is the head of the doctors of this hospital. He had a long talk with Jhimli. I couldn't hear what he said but could clearly see that again and again his gaze was coming to back to the well shaped breasts of my wife.

I could not locate my son. Definitely his lordship is yet to arrive from the States. Then I asked the haggard looking man accompanying me, "Then should I understand that I have expired? And you are the God! But people say that there is no God and it's only a dumb belief"

The man again gave the half-way-through smile. He replied, "Yes, you have expired and I am God. But people's scepticism is nothing wrong either. You can say I am sort of like the clerk working in the docks. I only record what comes in and what goes out. I have no power whatsoever."

I said, "Well, got it. But after all you can delay the despatch. I know these tricks. Once I did lose a big contract to Star Engineering. I sprang into action and as a result the goods were despatched late. The company had to pay heavy penalty and as a result rendered sick. Later on I bought the company at throwaway price. The dockyard clerks had a big role to play in my game."

The man said, "Yes I can delay your departure but I don't think that will be of any help"

- Why do you say so?
- Because you won't be able to do anything you are used to
- Drinking?
- Ruled out...you will receive some fluid through tubes, these fluids are tasteless and you cannot feel the taste of anything anyway.
- Womanizing?

- Sort of 'yes'...whole day nurses will take care of you just like a new born child has to be cared for..They will not even consider you as a conscious person.... so much so that at the end of duty hours they will change in front of you. And even if you figure in their discussions it is unlikely that they will romanticize about you. Does it seem okay?

I had nothing to say. Only a few day's back my partner Prabir's wife has said, "Samrat you are a tiger in the bed, compared to you Prabir is just dead meat".

So I said, "Not done, let me say good bye then."

The man said, "There is no hurry. I can spare few hours. During this period you can enter or come out of that cage with tubes attached, and then we will have to go."

I was little surprised and asked, "Why are you so generous? The only thing I have done well is provide jobs to some men; they say I am their God as I provide them bread. Is this the reward for providing breads?"

He jumped up and said, "No not all, actually this is the great convenient mistake?"

- Mistake?
- Since the creation of man I have planted a few virus circuits in the head. So people are unable to see the truth. They think you provide them bread and do not realize that the truth is other way round.

- What nonsense! I pay them; they are at my beck and call...
- True but the real work is done by them. You sell their toil and finance your pomp and grandeur. They enable you to maintain a costly wife and even costlier a mistress.
- Well...suppose I accept the trash logic...now please say why you are so generous?
- The reason is simple...you are devil incarnate but at least you do not try to hide the fact from your own self or your peers.

I can now see that there is sudden flurry of activity around my body. Probably they have sensed something is wrong... terribly wrong. From the arrangements they have made it is clear the billing must be sky high. Prabir's wife Tanuja is trying to keep up the spirits of my wife Jhimli. Prabir is the technical asset of my company. He runs my company by his grab over engineering and technology and I keep his wife Tanuja happy by the most ancient technology in the world. Tanuja for some time had been insisting that i divorce Jhimli and marry her. I have given her my word that's what I am going to do and she has believed me. Prabir on the other hand is going to start the new assembly line soon. Once it starts my production volume will get doubled and per piece cost will get reduced by almost thirty percent. He is a real technology lover, absolutely oblivious of my plans of getting rid of him once the line starts.

In college we had to study a paper called 'technological methods'. I was inconsolably poor in studies. Once in viva voce our professor BPC said, "I know there is no meaning asking you any question...yet as it is my job I will have to ask something. Can you please say what is there in the subject 'Technological Methods'? My answer was prompt.

-    Sir, when people take, no logical methods, it is called 'Technological Methods'.

BPC gave me pass marks!

Probably he thought that having me in the class would mean the same torturous experience for another long year. But my respect for studies in general and technology in particular was summed up rather brilliantly in my answer. I had plans in place not only getting rid of Prabir but also I knew how to enjoy his wife without any string of promise attached. I have a fantastic collection of Tanuja's stills in mother naked state as well as videos. She has little alternative but to give in to sex slavery.

Some of the doctors are busy in some discussion of profound importance. Meanwhile I have flown to the lobby and seen that the newscaster repetitively talking of my serious condition. That haggard man said people in newspaper offices are busy in gathering information to write my obituary. That doctor with darkest halo walks towards 'me' with the gait of a supreme authoritative man. He calls my wife and declares in a guarded manner that I am no more. My wife proceeds closer to bed. I can understand that she is trying to control her emotions.I cannot help playing a little prank. I slid into my 'mortal remains' and move a finger. Jhimli gives a short cry and loses consciousness. The dark halo doctor supports her and she is carried out. Now there is fresh spurt of activities. I know the concern written deep on their faces is actually synthetic. They are happy that the billing is not stopping right away and for a few more days at least this hospital will be in the focus of the electronic and printed media. A junior doctor is pushing some shots in the channel made in my right arm. I have checked the cost of one shot is more than what I pay to most of my staff as a month's salary.

Oh...I can see my son Anirban has arrived. The bustard comes close to 'me', stops for a second and then goes back. I can see that he takes his sister aside. There is quite a crowd outside now. I can see my friends from various clubs have arrived. A minister has also arrived with his pilot car, hooting and startling the visitors. He is also quite concerned. I understand his concern. He is yet to receive his 'commission' for a government contract that was decided in favour of a company owned by me. My departure would mean vaporization of five hundred million for him.

I can see my friends from the clubs deeply engrossed in discussion about the future of my companies. It is an open secret that my son and daughter are neither capable nor interested in running the show. So what the 'clubbers' are thinking but not uttering is who can buy which company of mine and at what price. They all know that all my companies are teeming with orders and recession means nothing to me. I have got no union problem in this Left ruled state where the most revered word is 'strike' and state wide strike or 'bandh' is performed periodically with the seriousness and devotion matched only by pilgrims when they set on a difficult venture. I regularly play good donations to the parties and also sponsor trips of the leaders to Singapore and Bangkok. Proximity to unclothed women rekindles the fire of revolution in them. And for quick recharge I have my resort at Panihati always ready for them.

I am deeply sensitive and respectful of the practices performed by the kings and noblemen in ancient India. They used to keep a stock of beautiful women who were systematically poisoned by expert doctors having infinite mastery on the subject. The poisons did no harm to these women but they were lethal to those who, allured by their charms took them to bed. The kings used them to kill high profile 'guests'. I also have a beautiful woman in my payroll. One union leader tried to double cross me and I used this lady. Few days back the union leader has breathed his last. His ill fame of course preceded his death as the news of his HIV infection was beautifully planted among his fiery comrades and of course in the media.

So I go ahead with retrenchment of the workers with the peace of mind even the Buddhist monks would envy. Make them work with dangerous chemicals without the bare minimum protective measures. I simply make a mockery of the rules laid out by pollution control board. And when I feel that things are may go wrong I offer a new 'scheme' of benefits to my workers. And with these titbits of benefits I keep them under my shoes. If the tsars of Russia could master this tactics they would not come such a cropper in the revolution because there would not have been any revolution.

Visiting hours is over and so everyone is being requested to leave. Given the criticality of the patient someone from the family is required to be at the lobby at night. There is nobody to volunteer. Jhimli cannot stay as she is not feeling well. My son is complaining of jetlag and needs to sleep. My daughter has a strong excuse as she has left behind her kid in charge of maidservant who leaves at night. After her divorce a few months back she is a single mother now. So they all leave, leaving me alone.

* * *

I come out of my form and find that ramshackle man sitting in a stool and dozing just like security staff in government offices. He blinks at me and asks, "Can we go now?"

I said, "No a little while more..."

He says, "But by tomorrow morning we must leave or we will be marked 'late'. It seemed highly ridiculous to me. "I am 'late' anyway since I am dead, so what late marking are you talking of?" I added, "By the way do you know why dead people are referred to as 'late'? I have never found the reason anywhere."

He said," Oh! That's simple. Actually 99.99999% people actually are dead by the time they are thirty or at most forty. Dead because after that they have no hope, no aspiration and no mission, yet they come to Hades when they are

seventy or eighty. Since they have not reported in time they
are called 'late'.

I said, "Okay you continue your nap, I will make a round."
He said, "Yep...I have to find a place to lie down in peace.
I have got rheumatism since last five thousand years and
need to stretch my legs. But it is so difficult to find a quiet
corner in the hospital at night; so many people become so
romantic".

* * *

I have come to my daughter's flat.

Beautifully decorated and very spacious it is. I bought it
during her marriage. But everything cannot be bought.
The marriage lasted only three years. That anyone could
muster the courage to divorce my daughter was beyond
my comprehension. The guy used to work in my company
when the marriage took place. After the trouble with my
daughter he left and joined another company, innocent of
the fact that I am a board member of his new employer. I got
him neatly framed with charges of pilfering with company
secrets and he was put behind the bars. Presently he is out
in bail and his career is more than finished. He spends his
time in cheap taverns.

I leave my daughter's flat presently. My son and daughter
are engaged in high pitched quarrel about the possession of
the wealth I am leaving behind. They know I have made no
will, so deeper they dig, bigger will be the pound of flesh.
I stood awestruck for a while hearing the filthy fight. Their

language would put the slum dwellers to shame. But at least in two points they are unanimous.

One – their mother must not get more than peanuts

Two – Old age home is the right place for her.

I drifted to my own home. There is pin drop silence everywhere. Even the servants' quarters are dark. My dear grey hound is sleeping on the carpet in my study. It is sleeping like the common mongrels on the road. It seems nobody had bothered to serve him food. I knew that the so called friends and relatives are of no use but didn't think that they are so hopeless. Someone should have volunteered to stay with my wife at least for this night. So everything they say is just lip service!

I was supposed to go on a Europe tour next week with Jhimli. God knows how much money the tour operators will return. My father was teacher of English in a small suburban school and used to read a lot. He had great desire for going to UK. When I returned from my first trip to UK he started asking me meticulously about all the famous spots, like Tower of London and Stratford on Avon. My short reply, "I have seen them all father" undoubtedly disappointed him. But the truth would have been harsher. Actually I had spent whatever leisure time I could manage in Soho, the infamous red light area of London.

I can see a little ray of light at the bottom of the curtain. That means the bedside lamp is on. That means Jhimli is awake, she cannot sleep without pitch darkness. What should I do? Should I go to her and tell that I have left her forever?

No, I cannot go. Not because she will be scared. But for the fact that she is not alone, someone has after all volunteered to stay with her for the night.

Two naked bodies are intertwined with each other like two snakes making love! It's obvious that Jhimli and Prabir are quite used to sleeping with each other. I can see the tour operator's catalogue at the side table, with some new markings. They have extended the programme to include the famous romantic spots.After all honeymoon without marriage is far sweeter than conditional honeymoon that comes with marriage.I need to leave. The sight and sound of what is going on are telling on me.

*   *   *

Morning in hospital is always a great flurry of activity. I come to my guide in rags and tell him, "let's go."

He says, "Will have to wait a bit. There is a problem with the link, the signal is too weak. The terrorists have blasted a few bombs resulting in lot of deaths, they have to be transported en masse, so facing problem with bandwidth as well."

This is not visiting hour, yet a lady has come to see me and is pleading with the staff. She says she is coming from quite a long distance and wants to be inside only for five minutes. She is clad in very ordinary half clean clothes, and carrying a bag in her shoulder. If observed one can understand that she was not bad looking twenty five or thirty years back but now poverty and hardship have taken their toll. Surprisingly enough, she seems familiar to me, a face I have seen recently, but cannot remember. It's quite embarrassing as I boast of my memory which, I believe, is quite photographic in nature. Secondly a woman of such attributes does not come close to me except in charity functions and I never bother to remember the recipients of alms who come to the charity functions.

The lady has real convincing power as she has managed the security and the hospital staff and is now seated next to my bed. She is looking at my face with unwavering stare with tears rolling down her cheeks.

Oh my God! This is Rini, and yes of course I know her. Her father was the compounder of the only qualified doctor we had in Bankura in those days. We called him Harikaka. Rini and Harikaka lived in a thatched hut behind the field of Christian College. Rini was my first love, in her I discovered what a woman is.

I can still remember all the details from that day. I had passed out from engineeringcollege and joined a service and Rini was then teacher in primary school. It was monsoon. I had gone home as there was some holiday or something. We were alone in their hut as Harikaka had gone to visit some relative. It was raining heavily and the rain drops on the tiles were creating a strange environment. The windows were lashing against the walls as the gusts of wind forced their way into the small room just like a plough plunders into the soil and makes virgin soil upturned.

And virgin soil was upturned. Rini surrendered to me.

Unfortunately the matter became known to others. Naturally I refused to marry Rini. Harenkaka committed suicide to escape the shame. I had to bear some expenses to avert trouble. Rini did lose her job in school. My father became extremely upset. But a master orator as I always was, I convinced him that it was only a ploy to malign me. What proof do these people have against me?

No, even if she had had any proof against me, she never came forward with it. My father summoned her to have a word, she didn't turn up. Probably this is a singular incident in his long life as teacher my father saw a student not listening to him. After that because of the ill reputation the incident endowed her with, Rini never got chance to get married.

It's Rini's face that flashed in my mind when I was struck by the acute piercing pain in my chest, not this face, but the way Rini looked thirty years ago. I now realize that I had never actually forgotten her. She still lives alone and is now coming from far away Bankura seeing my news in some newspaper.

Suddenly I feel turmoil deep within me, hitherto unknown. I don't know myself now. I wish I could stop this twister within, but i can't. I went to that man and said, "I don't want money or sex or anything just allow me to spend some days with Rini!"

He nodded disapproval.

"Then at least allow me a few days so that I can legally transfer a share of my huge wealth to her. She can lead a decent life."

He smiled a clear smile this time for a change.

"She leads a decent life. Rather you should think what sort of a life your huge wealth has given you."

I cried out in anger, "Why are you so heartless?"

He laughed, "Heartlessness is you monopoly Mr Samrat Chatterjee. You thought you had the right to defame an unsuspecting lady and that you have done fully, but who told you that you have the right to insult her with alms? You don't have that right great entrepreneur. She has fought a long lone battle and she can fight the rest. Today's generation is a different generation. They have not shunned her like their fathers did. She is highly respected social worker now. Don't confuse her social work with the social work of giving away old clothes as done by your wife's Ladies Club. She teaches the ladies of the village how to live with honour."

It becomes clear that there is nothing I can do.

So I said, "Please tell her to keep her palm on my forehead and to forgive me."

The man said almost in a soliloquy, "This is one of the wonders of the world, one who cannot recognize monumental generosity is also forgiven."

Rini places her palm on my forehead, the storms abate.

Like a movie I can see the first day I saw her, she was then a child of ten or eleven years. She was doing her studies in the light of a lantern.

She was reading a poem and learning it by heart.

"Darkness descends in the garden as the sun sets,
The water of the ponds now looks like ink,
The boatmen are back from the harbour
The farmers are back from the fields..."

Rini realizes that I am no more.
The forehead is cold.
Somehow she checks herself from breaking into tears and leaves the room in quick steps.

I approach God, and say, "Let's go"

The Stag Party

I never find a compassionate soul in my wife.When, almost as a regular ritual, I volley abuses about my job and my employer, my wife Paramita, seems to enjoy my outbursts. One day being unable to take it any more I accosted her and said "See, it's plainly inhuman! Your husband is withering out doing this lousy job and you are not a bit sympathetic!"

She smiled and said, "Had I not known you too well may be you could expect a sympathizer in me. But unfortunately I know that theseoutbursts against your job and again enjoying the little small successes on your way are actually means of your sustenance. Without these you cannot live a day. So when I find that you are 'angry' and declaring that you are going to resign I feel that the world is running smooth".

Paramita is correct, rather quite brutally so. So I keep on grumbling like a child who knows he has yet to learn the game but sulks at the fact that he cannot be the winner. The company I work for has bagged a job in Saudi Arabia and I will have to go to Al-Khobar to attend the kick-off meeting. So basically I was quite happy. I did actually plan to break the good news of my first foreign trip masking my elation. But my observant wife foiled my attempt at the very onset.

Well, it's time to introduce myself. I am Pradip Sen, forty and happily married with a daughter, and working in a construction company in middle management capacity. Paramita is of course happy to hear the news. She is a very balanced person and do not belong to the category of 'never satisfied' people. She is happy with what comes her way and seldom laments what she has lost.

But after some time I find that I am a bit worried. Honestly I would have been happier if my first foreign trip was happening to some other country. I feel I need some first-hand feedback from someone who has visited the place in recent past. As far as my knowledge goes none of my friends have visited Saudi Arabia and as this is our first project there I couldn't expect much help from my colleagues. I raise my concern at the lunch room. My colleague Joydeep blurts out, "Pradip you can only do your job but honestly you are far from smart". Joydeep's 'honest' remarks are always cutting but we have learnt to ignore the edges. So I calmly ask what is it he is trying to say. He says, "Talk to Debargha Roy of Purchase Department, he has worked there for many years, you will get what you are looking for."

I can remember the man. If there is a contest of how much low profile a man can maintain in an office, Debargha Roy is the sure winner. He is the most silent man I have ever seen in my office. Once I had to make a journey in train with him to one of our project sites. It lasted about four hours. But during our onward or return trips Debargha never used more than mono syllables for conversation. He seems even more out of place in our farm because here the general mood is very loud and quite garrulous. Even there is a notion that ability to shout at the top of thevoice in telephone is regarded as attributes for securing positive appraisals.

Next day during the lunch hours I visit the Purchase Department. Given the nature of Debargha I had construed that he prefers a quiet lonely lunch and not the din and bustle of the canteen. I was right. Debargha is having lunch at his table. I didn't miss that it is lunch brought from home and consists of handmade bread and some vegetable curry. Things seem quite to be in order. Debargha chewing a chicken leg would have been out of place. I introduce myself and say what I need from him. He stares at me for some time. When in fact I have started feeling a bit awkward he blurts out, "No never...I have never gone to that country...I have never gone outside Kolkata...you are wrong Sir". Naturally I had to get up. I apologise for disturbing him and leave. He doesn't seem to hear anything. Before passing through the door I look back and find that he is still lost in thought.

Later on I enquire about him and find that in general he is laughing stock. His initials DS (for Debargha Sen) has a different meaning for colleagues in his department; they understand DSstands for 'Deleted Self'. I could not help appreciate the name in spite of the gross lack of compassion. It really seems that for Debargha his own presence is the biggest concern. Somehow if he could live a life unheard or unseen by others he could have breathed at ease. Also interestingly I find that nobody is aware of anything about his personal life.

Anyway my problem gets solved as I come to know of a cousin brother of my wife Paramita who had been to Saudi. He gives me some necessary and more unnecessary information of the land and I prepare for the trip. But being unable to forget the episode of Debargha I keep on contemplating on the matter. Suddenly an idea dawns on me. I approach an acquaintance of mine, Shyamal who is a senior clerk in the HR department. I request him to show me the personal file of Debargha Sen.

Such requests are not uncommon to Shyamal but always such requests involve some single woman and not a nondescript like Debargha. Shyamal is naturally curious and his curiosity takes the form of a silly joke when he asks me whether I am considering Debargha Sen as would be son-in-law. I ignore the question as I have to keep my cool and get hold of the information i am seeking.

The information comes as a big shock.

Debargha Sen has worked in a city of Saudi Arabia for nearly four years!

I have heard that any indecent gesture to any woman can subject a man to merciless lashings in KSA. But given the persona of Debargha Sen it is too much to imagine that he is making advances towards any woman of that country. In fact I believe for Debargha making advances towards his own wife came as an obligation rather than a pleasurable proposition. Then what did happen in Saudi Arabia that makes Debargha so secretive about that period? No, he didn't get involved in any sort of scam. His release letter clearly praises his contribution to the company. Then why did he leave at all? He was in a much better position and his earning per month was almost equivalent to his yearly earnings now.

Anyway I proceed to my trip and almost forget about Debargha and his strange behaviour. Al-Khobar is a nice city by the sea. When I landed at Dammam airport I was immediately reminded of the story in Mahabharata where the demon Moy had created a fantastic palace for the Pandavas. There is a twenty five km long bridge over the sea that connects Al-Khobar with Bahrain. I also had some business to do in Bahrain and the drive on the long causeway is a fabulous experience. On my return flight my next seat is taken by a stately looking gentleman, Al Abbasi.

Abbasi loves to talk and talks nice. He offers me his visiting card. The name of the company and the logo strikes a bell. But I cannot recall where I have seen this logo. Then, having nothing better to do I tried to concentrate on a Hindi movie offered by the airlines which proved to be very much conducive to sleep and I dozed off. When I wake up I suddenly remember where I have seen this logo. I ask Abbasi if he can remember some Debargha Sen who used to work in this company. Abbasi looks at me for a long time and then admits that he knew Debargha. I added that Debargha Sen is now my colleague. For the rest of the journey Abbasi seem to recoil inside a shell and says nothing.

In Mumbai he walks very fast and stands much ahead of me in the immigration line and by the time I go past the immigration desk he has vanished. The other noteworthy issue of the journey was Indrani Basu. Indrani Basu is a very famous activist for women's causes and she is particularly busy fighting for the women of the Arab world. An airhostess informs that like me she will catch the flight to Kolkata from Mumbai.

Abbasi's behaviour adds to the big question mark called Debargha Sen. But I forcefully wipe out the queries. There are many curiosities which accompany us to the grave, unanswered of course. I understand curiosity about Debargha falls in that category. The man is too uninteresting to be curious about whatever may his background be.

In our office, like in many other offices, there is a tradition of having an annual function. This function as it happens everywhere starts with the speech of the top management. We call this time for exercise of the jaws as we all keep ourselves busy in a series of yawns. This is followed by even more boring session when some awards are distributed and speech of the guest of honour. Then of course there is a cultural function where professionals perform and that of course is normally enjoyable. In the preparatory meeting for this function I suggest the name of Indrani Basu as the guest of honour. Probably as I had her as co passenger in the flight she was there in my thoughts. It felt good when I later came to know that my suggestion has been accepted and Indrani Basu has been invited to chair the function. She indeed does it very gracefully. There is something in her personality that elicits respect but that something is never too pronounced.

The incident happened A few days after the function. As usual I was returning from office in my motorcycle when I found a gathering of an odd sort by the road. From a distance I could make out a gentleman was lying on the sidewalk. Since normally we lead a very mundane life subconsciously we always look for some spice particularly if it comes free. It is that craving for some happening that make us curious and I stop my bike, get down and move forward to explore the scene. To my utter surprise that the man is Debargha! A tea vendor and a few bystanders told me the story. Two young ladies waiting for a bus were being constantly pestered by street Romeos. Their indecent behaviour was not limited to mere words. We, the people of the city love to read news of such things in the comfort of home and enjoy them even more if little flavour of politics can be added. But we never like to protest and get involved in potential troubles. Debargha was passing by and unlike others he went forward and confronted them. As courage begets courage his action prompted others to join him and seeing trouble the Romeos chose to sprint.But as Debargha was blocking their way they gave him a hard push and while falling Debargha hit his head in the base of a lamp post and lost his consciousness.

Naturally I had to volunteer a bit of nursing to help him regain consciousness and accompanied him to his home. However, what suddenly turned a docile soul like Debargha into a righteous man remained a mystery. One good thing happened of course. When my colleagues came to know of the episode they stopped making fun of him.

The Durga Puja followed soon and like others I start enjoying riddance from office. But the problem of any festivity is the anticipation of the ensuing festival is much better than the festival itself because actual celebrations seem to pass too quickly. Dashami is the last day of the festival when the idols are immersed in the river Ganges. Quite unexpectedly a heavy downpour started and I was left with no option but to lock myself at home and watch immersions in the TV.

Paramita announced that I have a visitor. Who in right frame of mind would step out of home on such a day – I thought. To my surprise it was Debargha. He has come to visit me with a box of sweets. I did never hear nor could I imagine Debargha socialising with anybody so the whole thing seemed quite out of place.

"I need to be alone with you for some time" said Debargha without much of a preamble. I told him that it is okay. Actually the old curiosity raised its head.

I am presenting what Debargha said in his own words –

> First of all I must say I am deeply indebted to you for helping me that day. I have lied to you about my Saudi stay. I know you have done your homework and checked my CV from HR people. Today you are going to hear something which I have suppressed from most of the world. I was employed in a good company in AlKhobar, the city that you visited. After afew years of my stay I married Tuku, my childhood friend and my first love. Very few people in the world are lucky enough to marry their first love and probably that's precisely the reason stories like Devdas are so popular. The first year after marriage passed like fairy tale. But then I had

forgotten that the same fairy tales are the homes of demons as well.

I was in Purchase Department and there was a man called Hanif who reported to me. Hanif was outright dishonest and upon my report to the higher authorities Hanif was sacked. The guy who replaced him was called Rashid. I did of course realize that in the process of getting Hanif sacked I have created some enemies in the office. Rashid, the new chap, was quite young and jovial. One day I did invite him to dinner at my home and my wife Tuku also liked Rashid for his pleasant personality.

One of our clients, a big sheikh did invite some of the officers to his residence (you can think 'palace') on the occasion of Ramadan. The invitations were for couples. I arrived with Tuku in my Kia Car.

I didn't know that an embarrassment of a sort was waiting for me. We found that none of the other guests have come with their wives and Tuku was the only woman in the party. I did also observe that I was the only Indian invited, all others were locals. Rashid told me in a hushed tone, when he took me aside, that I had misunderstood, from the beginning it was planned to be a stag party. I felt rather like a fool after making the blunder. My immediate inclination was to apologise to the host and leave with Tuku.

Debargha stopped for drinking water. Then he sipped the remaining tea in the cup and resumed his story.

- But the Sheikh won't allow that. He said that we were his honoured guests and leaving like that would be severely against the tradition of eastern hospitality. He called his wife and asked her to take Tuku inside till the end of the party. Tuku was not exactly interested and nor was I but given the situation we both accepted the arrangement. What followed were sumptuous meals, music and drinks. Some of the dancers were there to entertain the men. Officially liquor is banned in Saudi but in certain places, like this one it flows like water. When the party ended I requested the Sheikh to call my wife from inside as we need to leave, and of course thanked him for everything. Sheikh was highly astonished.

- He said 'But you have come alone!'

  And everybody else present in the party, all my long time colleagues, seconded the opinion of the Sheikh. They made fun of me and said that I have drunk too much; I should drive cautiously and go home where my wife is waiting for me. I was furious...I ran to the police. Police asked for witness as without a witness they cannot lodge a complaint against such a 'big' man. And there was no witness. Even the security staff, the valet who parked my car all vouched that I had gone alone.

I sought help from the Indian embassy but they were all tied by the intricacies of law. I did write to the government in India but they asked me to depend on the Embassy in Riyadh. I did seek help from my top boss who was an American but all he could do is to get the case lodged as a common missing diary. I know had I been some celebrity or apolitical person of importance the embassy would have acted otherwise but unfortunately I wasnot. As an irony of fate the same year the King of Saudi Arabia was the honoured guest in the Republic Day Parade of India.

Of course by this time I had collected some more information. But the information had come too late. The sheikh was notorious in close circles for his penchant for good looking young women and Rashid is half-brother of the corrupt Hanif who was sacked. I did try and try to find Tuku for a year and then returned to India. I could not breathe in Al Khobar anymore.

Debargha stopped. It is still raining outside. A strange but very strong feeling of insecurity had grasped me while hearing the story of Debargha. A man can lose his loved wife like this! I am also a family man with a daughter. I got up and came to the room where Paramita was sitting watching television with my daughter. However foolish it may be I think I needed to be sure that my loved ones are still there safe and sound. Paramita asked whether In needed more tea or something. I barely answered and came back to

Debargha. He was sitting just as I had left him. Is Tuku still a sex slave in that palatial hell of the sheikh?

-       Tuku managed to escape that palace after two years.

I was little startled. It seemed as if he has read my mind.

-       She came back to India. We met in a small cafe. These two years I have been constantly tormented by repentance. Repentance at the thoughts why I did take her to the party or why I didn't summarily leave with her when I saw it was a stag party. These were mistakes, deadly mistakes yes, but not crimes. But when she met me and wanted to resume her normal life with me, almost begged me for a chance of normal life – I did commit a crime, the biggest crime of my life. I told her the chapter is closed, I cannot accept her as my wife any more. I didn't know why I did so, or what the problem was ...but I was stern. She left without a further word. After some time I received the divorce notice in mail. After the process was over I got into manic depression which will accompany me to the funeral piers. I have to take eleven medicines every day. It's simply God's grace that I have been able to retain my job. I have retreated inside a tortoise shell. I know I am a laughing stock but I don't dare to step out. But that day, when I found those boys heckling the two women, suddenly they reminded me of the Sheikh. My Tuku was of the same age as those two women. I couldn't hold back myself. You helped me a lot that day so I thought it's my duty to tell you everything. Otherwise what people think about me matters nothing. After that evening in the party I can believe nobody.

I will have to go now. I think the rain has stopped. Please tell your wife I enjoyed the tea and chicken nuggets. And will be glad if you keep the story to yourself.

I could not help asking the question which was intriguing me for some time.

- Do you know the whereabouts of Tuku, your wife I mean?
- You all know her. She is a big figure in International circles. She works for women's rights. Her name is Indrani Bose, Tuku was her nickname. We are in touch. In fact I did request her to chair our office function. Well I have medicines to take. The office reopens tomorrow; I will have to get up in time. Good bye.

The Incurable

Ashim was my batch mate in engineering college. I can almost vouch that he was one of the, if not the most unpopular chap in the class. Everybody is not rowdy but at that age somewhat challenging attitude is of course expected from boys particularly from the boys of engineering college. But Ashim was exceptionally docile and that made him the odd one out. Whether someone snatched his cigarette he had just lighted or take away his imported clutch pencil and hand him a blunt shabby pencil, he would not react at all.

Once, just before the semester examinations he borrowed a book from me for photocopying the relevant chapters. After he left with the book I remembered that we two had bought the same book together from the same shop. When he came to return my book I asked what the matter was, had he lost his copy.His answer was equally funny and infuriating. Many students from so called backward states and countries used to come to study in our college. They were always endowed with more than handsome scholarships and rarely did they complete their course in time. One such student had 'borrowed' his book and meek as he was, he could never get back the book. I was mad on hearing this and remember saying that had I known all these I would not have allowed him to get chapters from my book photocopied. After getting my thrashing Ashim murmured, "You see I can manage the exams with the photocopied chapters. I had a doubt about that boy while lending the book but after all they are our guests you see...Can you give them a 'no'?"

Given our age we were rightfully interested about our young ladies. Some of us were having regular affairs. Quite naturally they were sort of elite amongst us. Pornographic literature was in high demand. Since internet was not known in those days, books printed in poor newsprint quality paper and shoddily bound were the only recourse. And also women were the most favoured topic in idle gossips. One thing I did notice. Ashim never participated in these 'girly' discourses and whenthese gained momentum he used to leave the gathering silently. This was noticed by others as well and it is easily imaginable what sort of branding did this so called lacks of interest in women earn him.

Ashim was quite handsome and used to always dress in well maintained clothes. Once lady scholar of Arts called Pallavi did send him a letter. For one whole week following the incident Ashim was absent from class. It was reported that he had high fever. In short he was considered weird and as nobody easily befriends people like him he was sort of a loner. So after finishing college and entering professional lives none of bothered to maintain contact with him though we knew that he is living in Kolkata and working in such and such company. It was unthinkable to expect Ashim to voluntarily call anyone of us and re-establish contacts and that unthinkable thing never happened.

Then one day I did meet Ashim, some twenty years after leaving college. I was on my way to home from office and saw a crowd in the midst of the road. It seemed a sort of squabble is going on. Normally I do not take interest in such matters but that day I alighted from my car and went ahead to get the details. A bike with a pillion rider has taken a sudden right turn without the necessary indications and the car just behind it has somehow managed to stop to avoid a serious collision. The bike riders instead of apologising for their mistake and thanking the car for managing to avoid a catastrophe were attacking the car driver in filthiest of language possible. The owner of the car who was driving the car was standing beside the car and trying to face the volley of obscenities with feeble words of self-defence. I saw that it was Ashim and understood these long twenty years has not changed our batch mate.

In Kolkata a lot of bystanders are always available as the unemployed population is huge. They were present and almost all of them were supporting the errant bikers. Naturally I had to step in and close the nonsense show. Then Ashim and I entered a shanty teas stall nearby to have a few words.

Ashim said that he was married with a son and had already lost his mother. Their ancestral home had been demolished and high-rise apartment stood there. Ashim lived with his wife, son and old father in one of the apartments of the building. He did insist very much to visit his family and almost made me promise to go there soon. The fact that

Ashim was insisting on anything and that too so steadfastly was so astonishing that I conceded.

Ashim's wife Mimi was a teacher in a school. She was quite suave andwell kept. She had a pleasant disposition. She expressed that she was bored and tired of teacher's job and wished to migrate to corporate world. Their only son Rintu was twelve and seemed rather too quiet for a boy of his age.

Just two days after this I had a surprise visitor in my office, Mimi. It was around five in the evening. Not that I am unused to visitors but normally they are always scheduled by appointments. Also Mimi did never show any inclination about coming to my office. I sat with her in our visitor's room and asked the tea boy to serve coffee for us. After a few minutes of small talk Mimi asked, "Would you mind if I request you to call it a day and then we go out?"

Though I didn't support the idea exactly, curiosity got better of me and I conceded.

-    Where do you want to go? I asked
-    I think we can decide that once we start.

We drove towards City Centre two. They have a few good joints in City Centre two. During the drive Mimi was mostly doing the talking. What I could gather, and it was very easy as she was quite repetitive, she wanted me to understand that she was not happy.

As courtesy demanded I had to ask the actual reason for her ill being,

She answered, "You know your friend, and do you think the company of so docile a person can be enjoyable?"

I sensed that it was unethical, even though mildly, to discuss my classmate with his wife. So to makemood lighter I said, "But I knew women like good boy husbands. In fact there are so many cases where loud and demanding husbands are reported against to the law."

My attempt at cutting a joke fell flat. I made an attempt from another angle.

- But you have a beautiful son. Doesn't he occupy lion's share of your time and attention?
- Please don't talk like an old man Arnab" said she "I am of course a loving mother, but don't you think I can crave for love from the man in my heart"

We make tall talks about and essentially against male chauvinism but deep down we are all chauvinists, at least I am a chauvinist for sure. Unfriendly words from Mimi and sudden lack of proper argument made me rude.

I said, "Of course you can crave for love from the man in your heart. But from your account so far it doesn't seem that Ashim is that man. It is quite possible that you are also not the woman in his heart."

She remained silent and sullen. By this time we have reached the parking lot of the mall. We got out and came to a small but daintily decorated restaurant. I was, honestly speaking a bit ashamed at my sudden 'show of strength' which was actually show of utter weakness. I ordered coffee and some light snacks.

Mimi opened her bag and took out a two page print out of her bio-data. She handed me the pages and said, "I know there are vacancies for a few secretaries in your office and I also know that you people attach a lot of importance on referrals. I need the job."

On hindsight I feel I should have avoided being nice to the lady. But actually I did submit the Bio-data with a note and in due course Mimi was called for an interview and subsequently she received the offer letter.I did take care though that Mimi joins insome other department and not where I work. I cannot pinpoint exactly but there was something in her that made me feel ill at ease. So I felt it was better to have her somewhere in the office where I would not be obliged to meet her every day. Ashim did call and express his gratitude for the help. He was in fact insisting on another visit which I took care to avoid.

The entire episode had started moving into oblivion when, quite unexpectedly, I was forced to feel guilty for two happenings. Ashim's son was diagnosed with Autism. Ashim did insist that Mimi leave the job as his son needed full time care. Mimi didn't listen. She was quite 'enamoured' with the charms of building a career. Very soon it became clear that Mimi had chosen a sort of 'fast track' for her career advancement. Mimi had been assigned the job of secretary of one Mr. Joshi who too interested in exploring women. To keep his life unencumbered so that he could pursue his interest Joshi had not tied the knot and lived alone with servants in a villa.

Mimi started accompanying this Mr. Joshi in all office tours. And before long Mimi left Ashim and her son bag and baggage and shifted to the Joshi's villa.

My college friends knew the background of Mimi's joining in my company and quite naturally I had to bear quite a few unfriendly remarks from them after this. I went to Ashim one day. Told him that I was sorry and I shouldn't have jumped at the act of 'philanthropy'. I was ready for another volley of accusations from Ashim. But I had misjudged him.

He only smiled and said, "I don't see why you should be blaming yourself. She wanted a job and you helped her to get one. Even if you couldn't I don't think she would have given up the idea. She would have managed to get a job anyway. And all working women do not leave home to become their bosses' partners. It's in here Arnab" Ashim tapped his head, "...once one decides to leave she will leave, you can't keep someone tied down."

That day I dined with Ashim at his home. He said that he himself had cooked all the dishes! I must admit dinner on that day was far more enjoyable than the earlier occasion. When I asked how he was managing the show without Mimi and with the son who was quite ill he said that he had left his job and he was managing everything himself.

I was quite surprised to hear all these.

"But how will you manage? After all you need to earn" asked I. He said that he had got some investments that yielded regular returns, and also he had started a small consultancy business. To save cost he had sold off his car and now managed with a second hand scooter.

That night I returned home quite in a puzzled state. We often describe run of the mill films or literature as 'formula' work. But in actuality we all live by certain formulae which are written nowhere but very clearly etched in our minds. For example for a professional man it is expected that he will continue in the rat race whatever may be the circumstances. If Ashim had opted for a better paid job so that he could afford a full time nurses for his son and had continued in his journey of building his career that unwritten formula would have been satisfied. But leaving his job and choosing a Spartan life for the care of his son was very much 'out of the box'. Thinking deeply I realized that I was also not exactly enjoying the life I was leading. Like Joshi I had also not tied the knot, and had lost my parents long back. So I gave in to fantasy I had for long, I decided to settle in some foreign country.

It was not very difficult to find a job of my choice and I moved to the States. A few months after settling in Greenville I came to know that Joshi, as was only expected, had dumped Mimi and with neat manipulations had also managed to get her sacked from the company. There was nothing unexpected in this but can't say that I was not astonished to got a mail from a friend reporting that Mimi had gone back to Ashim. Ashim had accepted her and reinstated her with full honour.

I closed the computer after reading the mail, poured myself a big peg and thought that Ashim had lost whatever relics of a spine he had.

* * *

When I settled abroad I had plans of coming back in about five years. That five actually became fifteen and ultimately I returned after retirement. My employer did want me to continue as advisor but my inner self advised otherwise. So I came back and started working with an NGO who work in healthcare.

I had lost my parents years back and both had died in sudden heart failures. There was hardly any chance of medical attention. Fortunately I have enjoyed and still enjoy quite good health and so I had had no idea about the cost of medical treatments in my own country. Now working with this NGO I realize almost every day that huge advancement in medical care is practically of no use to the multitude of my countrymen as calling the costs prohibitive is height of an understatement.

Suddenly last night got the news that our college friend Ashim is no more. We all know that the only event in life that can be called inevitable is death, yet news of any death particularly of someone of our own age seems very unsettling. Was in no mood for dinner and decided to visit Ashim's house in the morning.

When I was getting ready in the morning got a call from Mimi. Ashim has left behind a letter for me! I was not in touch with him since I left for US and so it was quite a surprise.

The letter was in a sealed envelope with my name on it. I opened the envelope and found a single page letter written in quite neat handwriting.

It read

Dear Arnab,

I know my days are numbered. So it's high time to put a few things in black and white. You people always knew that I am a coward. You used to say that I can never protest. I fully agree with you as I always did. I believe it is a matter of bent of mindwhich cannot be changed. You can say sort of incurable. I know that you didn't like the fact that I did accept my wife when she came to back to me. Otherwise you would have dropped me a line or two at least once in a while.

Actually my son Rintu loved his mother very much. I could never bring myself to disclose to him the wrong doings of Mimi. You will call it cowardice and I do accept. But actually I felt it would be monstrous to shatter the colourful world of my son. I always used to tell him his mother had gone to some far away land and would come back one day. And then she really did come back. Honestly I had a very hard time and had to fight a tough private battle in accepting her. However, I did so for Rintu and of course for myself. You know I have always preferred the easy way out in my life.

Six months back I was informed that I have cancer in my cologne. It was already in quite advanced stage. I came to know of the huge costs I will have to incur for treatment. I knew the story that was going to follow, a long drawn and costly episode of treatment ending in funeral pyre. You know that I have left regular service long back and was sustaining on my own consultancy business. I have managed to make some savings for my son. With his illness he couldn't make it big in studies but fortunately is a gifted artist. He paints really well. But we all know that making a living from painting is not an easy proposition here. Whatever savings I have made would be lost in my treatment. So I decided that I will not go for any treatment.

You know Arnab; I feel that this so called advancement in science means nothing. What is the merit in advancement if a family has to come a cropper to get the fruits of so called successful research? And in true sense can we call this a civilization? Me, as a responsible father cannot make my son become a pauper for my selfish needs. I have never ever kept away anything from Mimi. But now I had to keep the news of my illness a secret. I knew that she won't be able to accept my logic.

I am very much indebted to my doctor as he helped me in keeping it a secret. He gave me medicines to enable me to bear the pain.

I can feel that time is drawing near. The painkillers are working no more. I just try to draw courage from a single thought. That thought gives me deep solace and strength. At least I have been able to make and preserve bare minimum provisions for my son and my wife.

I hear an election rally going past my house. These vote beggars come to us for votes and then simply forget us. The government has no actual concern for us so we have to provide for ourselves.

I know that you will understand me. Please be with my family. And please tell Mimi to forgive me for not going for any treatment.

I had no choice.

Yours truly,
Ashim

I read the letter twice and sat stupefied for long. I felt that Ashim has never ever stood up in protest. Perhaps he had reserved the strength in the core of his heart. Today with this silent departure he has registered a resounding protest against a huge wrong doing of the so called civilized advanced society.

To Achieve A Target

Grand Old man God is often in a very impish mood these days. While He is supposed to grant prayers of mere mortals he is doing so but doing it in the opposite. Supposing you see a bunch of good looking girls in the queue for getting boarding pass and assume by all probability one of them must be having the seat beside you in this boring long flight. God listens to your prayer and when you take your seat you find a grumbling old man beside you who is never tired of talking on boring topics and also snores. And the good looking ladies get seats around your boss.

Ambar is quite a helpful chap and has got the reputation of playing the Good Samaritan. He loves to do all sorts of jobs but has got a specific aversion towards visiting and spending time at hospitals. But this week He has sent him to the same hospital not once but thrice! First visit was to collect the report of some blood tests his father has to take regularly. The second visit was for prostrate operation one distant uncle was undergoing. This uncle has no issues and aunt is old and infirm. So Ambar had to do all the running around. And today he is here as a neighbour Feku Da has suffered multiple fracture of his right leg as he had a free fall from a guava tree in his premises.

By now it may seem to the readers that Ambar is a member of the few million strong unemployed brigade of Bengal. Actually it is not so. He has got quite a decent job in a well-managed company. In his company the leaves for the New Year are accrued on the 1st of April. He had some leaves from last year in his credit which he thought he would enjoy and so he had applied for the leaves.

"And this is how I am enjoying" sighed Ambar. He had planned complete rest, waking up late every day and reread the detective novels that occupy lion's share of his book case. Ambar can accept the previous two visits to this hospital. After all aged people will be sick and it's natural. But today's case is beyond any limit of tolerance. This Feku da who has broken his leg is really a crank. Theguavas in his tree are of exceptional quality. Even the birds do not bother to touch them. But he is undaunted. He will fetch the fruits, distribute them to the neighbours and even catch hold of boys playing in the streets and make them eat those delicacies! The boys normallyleave their playing gear behind and run for life at the sight of Feku approaching. But at times they have to concede as Feku da buys them cricket balls when they need. Feku da has lost his wife few years back. It is not known why suddenly she suffered so massive a stroke. Some people say falling prey to a sudden surge of marital love she had taken too many of those obnoxious fruits. Feku da is childless. So hearing his scream the neighbours had to rush. The others have cited office or other work and have left discreetly and Ambar became the odd one out. Ambar is thinking that unemployment is often cited as the biggest problem and the root of many other problems but if society didn't have an army of unemployed youth the problem it will pose would be even more difficult.

Anyway now the surgery is over. Ideally nobody needs to stay back in the hospital. But unfortunately it has been diagnosed that Feku has an ischemic heart and is suffering from an unstable condition since the fall. So the doctors have requested someone to be present in the lobby at least for a few hours. At this hour the waiting hall of any big hospital very closely resembles ashady cocaine joint. Most of the people are trying utmost to sleep. Some great men have actually gone to sleep and they are snoring, creating an uncouth combination of sight and sound. Everybody is basically disgusted because they have to stay back. People actually concerned for the sick and admitted are never present at this time. They are there at nights and at this hour they are almost forcefully taken away to homes to have some rest. Ambar never sleeps in the afternoons. He has learnt by heart almost everything printed in the magazine he is carrying. So in order to kill time Ambar started studying the people around. And then he noticed this man.

He realized he has seen him twice before.

On his first occasion Ambar had to wait long as the clerk who was supposed to despatch the blood report didn't come in time. There were some men and women around, seemingly relatives of some patient whose condition was critical. They were standing in a round and talking animatedly about the next possible course of action. And then Ambar saw this man for the first time. He was dressed in bright coloured shirt, even brighter tie and black trousers and was wearing a pair of sunglasses. None of the items of his attire were costly but since well-maintained he looked quite distinguished. Another interesting feature of the man is there was always a smile in his face which is quite inappropriate in a hospital lobby. At first Ambar did think the guy is a medical representative as only these men come to hospitals in snazzy attires. The man proceeded towards the animated group in small steps and asked what the crisis was all about. Crisis it was indeed as it was a case of burst appendix and the patient was a young man of twenty three only and was literally fighting for his life.

The man introduces himself as Somnath Sen and says to the eldest gentleman in the crowd, "Did you say Dr. Dasgupta is doing the surgery? Man you simply go home and relax. You are lucky that Dr. Dasgupta is handling the case. He is not human he is God! You don't know so many big hospitals around the world have generous standing offers for him. Vellore wants him as the head of surgery. But he won't go as he loves this city."

The elderly man was the father of the sick man. Quite naturally he was a bit glad to hear these words just like a drowning man feels charged to find a floating plank. To be more confident he asked, "How do you know so much about the surgeon Sir?"

"Of course I know...he operated on and saved my elder brother's son."
"What exactly was the problem in his case?"

"Don't ask me Sir...he had a nasty accident in his bike. Had a punctured spleen, and damaged pancreas. Other doctors practically asked us to contact the undertaker."

"How is he doing now? Leading normal life?"

"Normal life! He is regular soccer player in first division category. Within a few days he will be part of one of the big three soccer teams."

"That's great! By the way how about the facilities in this hospital? They have a well-equipped OT and all that?"

Now the man took some time to answer.

"Are you aware of the term medical tourism?" The elderly man is not quite conversant with modern terms and concepts.

"I mean...not exactly. Is it something like going to other countries?"

"No Sir" explained coloured tie, "Nowadays people from first world countries are coming to India to get world class treatment at one fourth of the cost."

"Really!" The elderly man suddenly lit up with enthusiasm.

"Yes Sir. Of course mostly the crowd is going to Vellore, Chennai, Miot Hospital etc."

"Yeah, Kolkata is not that good in..." the elderly man's enthusiasm was quickly dying out.

"Here...in this very hospital...apart from Vellore the only place where these foreigners are coming is this IRDS Hospital. Look...you see that gentleman? He is from USA and multi-millionaire...did come here for critical heart surgery and now is going back to lead a perfect normal life. When he was brought in, he was in ventilator."

The elderly man was greatly relieved. In fact he was almost jubilant.

"You give me great confidence man." said he.

Somnath Sen said that he was there as an elderly relative was undergoing prostrate surgery. Ambar next saw him when he came after fifteen days, and again he is there today. What can be behind this? Has this man dedicated his life for the well-being of his relatives and friends? And are his relatives and friends in some kind of hospitalization spree?

Ambar's train of thought is broken as a group seating near him has started a discussion on MRI scan. News has come from the ward that the doctor has prescribed the scan and the patient has to be moved to a clinic called Equinox nearby for getting the scan done. The transportation will be arranged of course by the hospital authorities. Somnath Sen approached the group in his usual measured steps.

- Excuse me, but can I talk with you for a minute?
- Yes...but please be fast. We are in the midst of an emergency.
- I know...and that's why I have approached you.
- What is it?
- I think you are taking you are patient to Equinox.
- Yes...we have been instructed to...
- You know something...your doctor, I mean Dr. Ghosal is a great physician but he has this problem.
- Yes Dr. Adinath Ghosal, you know him?
- Yes, last month he treated my elder brother's daughter.
- What is the problem?
- You do one thing...do not go to Equinox. You better go to MC Laboratories. It is much nearer. You will get much better job at half the price.

- What if the doctor doesn't like it?
- No issue, he will not mind. Actually it belongs to his relative so he is sort of obliged to advice Equinox. But he is a true gentleman and knows what is what.
- Thanks…thanks a lot…can you please give us the address of the lab you suggested?

So this man is a rare exception, thought Ambar. Normally such over friendly people are sources of botheration. But this gentleman is really trying to help unknown people! Ambar decides he must befriend this gentleman and know more about him. And luckily an opportunity gets created soon.

Ambar comes out of the lobby to smoke a cigarette and finds that his lighter has run out of gas. Somnath Sen is smoking nearby and at the same time talking in his cell phone. From his conversation Ambar comes to know that his nickname is Bheku. Once his call is finished Ambar approaches him for a strike.

He asks, "Hallo Sir, how is your uncle doing?"

"Sorry?" Sen is bit bewildered.

"I am asking how your uncle isrecovering. Didn't your uncle undergo prostrate surgery few weeks back?" asked Ambar.

"Oh yes yes…he is fine. But how do you know?"

"Actually I did come here some three weeks back and did overhear you saying someone of your uncle's illness. Glad to hear that he is doing fine"

"Oh thanks" Somnath stubs his cigarette and starts going back to the lobby.

"So why are you here this time?" Ambar is not really happy in ending the meeting.

"Oh nothing...just a small business." Says Somnath Sen and almost runs back to the lobby.

Ambar finished smoking and just as he is turning to go back to the lobby he notices something left on a table. Actually the hospital cafeteria is nearby and some tables and chairs are kept around for people to relax with coffee and snacks. On one such table Ambar finds a pair of specs. Surely Somnath Sen has left it behind. Ambar remembered that Sen was wiping his face with a handkerchief after finishing talking in the phone. Surely he has kept it there at that time.

Ambar picks it up. Now he must find the man and return it to the owner. Ambar, was going to keep the specs in his pocket when, God knows why, he brings it near his eyes and looks through the glass. A big surprise was waiting for him. He finds that the glasses are simple normal glasses having no ophthalmic value! That means Somnath Sen wears glasses just to look smarter. Though it is not extremely uncommon for people to wear glasses for cosmetic reasons, given the profile of Somnath Sen it seems really out of place, thought Ambar.

Ambar walks in but cannot spot Somnath Sen anywhere. So he leaves the glasses with the name and description of the owner at the hospital reception.

Being an addict of detective stories Ambar loves thinking that he himself has acquired some qualities of a sleuth. He can sense very well that there is something fishy about Somnath Sen and cannot forget the matter. He must get to the bottom of the matter and do so fast. He has got only two days of vacation left and once he joins back to work he cannot think of anything outside office.

Ambar has come to the MC Laboratories that Somnath Sen had prescribed to the elderly man. He is talking with the receptionist posing as relative of a fictitious man who needs to undergo certain tests. Suddenly two young gentlemen in blue uniform normally worn by orderlies embark from inside a room talking to each other.

One man is heard saying to the other,

"Do you know if Bheku is coming today? I did loan him five hundred bucks for two days and now it is nearly six months and he has not returned my money".

Ambar has got the gift of making quick plans just like copybook sleuths. He approaches the man and says, "Excuse me Sir, but can you please tell me the address of Bheku? Actually I did borrow two thousand bucks from him and I need to return the money. Unfortunately I have lost his phone number."

The man is clearly astonished.

"Bheku has given a loan to you!"

"Yes and actually I did promise to repay him within a week. It's more than a month now. It's highly unethical to delay any further." said Ambar.

The orderly calls a tea boy and says, "This boy will take you to Bheku's home. He lives nearby."

Ambar follows the tea boy to a nearby slum. He stops in front of a ramshackle hut and calls Bheku. Bheku comes out. He is clad in cheap and partially torn vest and shorts. He doesn't seem to be much surprised to see his visitor and calmly summons Ambar to enter the hut.

"I knew that you have understood that something is wrong. Actually my son is very sick, he is suffering from pneumonias, so you find me at home." said Bheku.

"Your real name is not Somnath Sen and you do not go to the hospital to visit any relative admitted there. Isn't it so?" Ambar directly comes to the point.

"You are right Sir. My name is Bhakta Das and people call me Bheku. I am an employee of the hospital. It's my job to talk with the relatives of the patients and make them feel confident about the hospital".

"And MC Laboratories and Equinox are owned by the same group who owns the hospital, right?" Ambar has done his homework well.

"You are right again, Sir." said Bheku, "Actually people are in a distressed state in a hospital. My job is to impart some confidence in them.

Actually hospital business is just like any other business. They have a sales target. All these are to achieve that target. But tell me, why did you come to suspect me in the first place?"

"You did make a small mistake when you tried to pass off a foreigner as a 'medical tourist'. Actually he is a world famous cardiologist who had come to the city for some seminar. I don't know what brought him to your hospital though. I saw his photo in the newspaper the next day."

A young girl, clad in equally torn frock brings tea for Bheku and Ambar. The cup and saucer are both partially broken. Bheku confessed that after unsuccessfully looking for a job for two years he was sort of forced to accept this job. He is a graduate. He knows that lying is bad thing but he is undone. Ambar hears from inside what seems like someone is coughing his lungs out. Bheku says that he is suffering from 'double pneumonia'. Ambar knows actual name of the disease is Pleural Pneumonia. The patient is Bheku's son aged about fifteen. Bheku has lost his wife few years back. She was crushed by a car driven by a bunch of drunken ruffians making merry on New Year's Eve. Nobody was booked.

The girl who served tea is Bheku's daughter. Ambar realizes that his mission is over. He almost forces Bheku to accept two five hundred rupee notes. It is quite clear that Bheku needs the money for paying off his debts and also for his son's treatment. The hospital pays only three hundred rupees for a day's work and there is no pay if he doesn't turn up for duty. Ambar tells the episode in MC Laboratory and how he managed to reach Bheku. Bheku requests to keep the matter a secret as otherwise he would lose his job instantly.

About a month or so later Ambar happened to visit the same locality for some personal work. Hedecided to pay Bheku a visit but found his shanty locked. Bheku has gone to work. Sunday means nothing to a man for whom no work means no pay. A neighbour told that his son did die a few days after Ambar's visit.

Ambar knows if he again has to go to IRDS Hospital he will find 'Somnath Sen' busy in his work.

May be he is comforting some worried father, "What did you say, complicated case of pneumonia? Oh man you are getting your son treated by Dr. Baidya here in IRDS and you are worrying! Hail God that you are here...relax man relax, take my word, you can assume your son is already cured. My son's case was far more complicated and now he is the University Blue!"

The Celebrity

When sub-editor Shishir summoned me in his cubicle and handed me a book and said, "I want the review within two days, word limit five hundred" I only humbly reminded him that the remunerations from past six book reviews are still due. I also thought that if I manage to get the seven remunerations together by another week that will help me paying the salary of my maid servant.

I am Satadal Roy. I have lost my parents years back, a bachelor by status, and live alone in my ancestral home in old part of the city of Kolkata. From very early age I attained sort of philosopher like insight of life and did become very much laid back in everything. My favourite phrase became, "What's the use?" So much so that my friends in my college used to call me "What's the use?". I often hear that Bengalis as a race are characterized by lack of ambition. If that is the trademark of Bengalis then I can be claimant of 'The True Bengali' award if there is any. In fact I had no intention of going to college and become a graduate. I did voice my apathy towards academic efforts to my father and my speech did end with my trademark dialogue. Unfortunately I was not taken kindly and my father unable to control his disgust slapped me with one of his huge slippers, so I had to go to college and get a Bachelor of Arts degree.

Then at one point of time I realized that the rent I receive from the two flats I have inherited may be enough to run a bachelor's life but I need to do something for an identity. So I chose the profession most suited for idlers like me. I became free-lance reviewer. Since I don't like doing anything original I have no paucity of interest in criticizing others. Most surprisingly now I am sort of a known name in literary circles. The other day I saw a gentleman has written in 'letters to the editor' praising my reviews and has used adjectives like 'unbiased', 'bold' etc. I wish my father could read them.

Anyway, leafing through this book I find that the author is one Jayanta Bhowmick. It is a posthumous publication that has seen the light of the day because of the efforts of Mr. Bhowmick's widow. Normally such self-publishedbooks are of very mediocre quality. At times they even fail to achieve mediocrity. At first I thought I will give it to my 'assistant' and ask him to brief me. Then of course I decided against it. Cheating someone who is alive is no big deal. I am also cheated by so many people and so often. But cheating someone who is no more did seem too unethical.

I have a habit of going to bed with a book. That night I decided to read the book of Jayanta Bhowmick. I found there were twelve stories in all. I expected to read a maximum of one or two as I was tired.

* * *

This maid of mine is serving for years now. My friends who frequent my house call her 'high frequency'. She has gifted voice that closely resembles the noise that would be created if several cracked gongs are hit together. On that morning her shouts in front of my main door had gathered a small crowd. The reason was simple. It was past nine in the morning and she had been banging my door for more than ten minutes (though she claimed it was more than thirty minutes) and still failed to wake me up. Fortunately I woke up, opened the door and requested her to stop talking and prepare tea. How could I make her understand that I was dragged through the pages reading in frenzy. I completed reading the book at about three AM. But I was awake for at least an hour more. The stories were making their rounds in the front and back parlours of my brain.

Bengali literature can boast of grand story tellers and great stories. But I doubt if I have ever come across so many good short stories in a single collection and that too written by an absolutely unknown author! In fact I felt sad that this book, sort of maiden venture by a man is also 'swan song' of the author as we can expect nothing from him in future.

The stories are all different in their subject matter. The smart style and intelligent economy of words can be enviable to so called established celebrity authors. The stories have been written over the years and though subtle, the changes taking place in the author can be identified. Something struck me as odd and to get the matter clarified I call Shishir.

Shishir is averse to taking calls in his off-days. However, my fourth attempt finds success. I ask him for the contact number of the author's wife.

"Why do you need to contact the author's wife to review his book?" Shishir is visibly disturbed and angry. Then perhaps he realizes that his tone was very rude. So to control the damage he tries to cut a joke "Is there any cryptic direction to treasure hunt in that book that you have deciphered? I deserve a share then!"

"No Sir. I just want to talk to the lady" said I.

"Oh…the man must have given very exciting description of his wife and that makes you so eager to meet her" Shishir is still not through with pulling my leg, "But one word of caution. These writers always write in hyperbole while writing about such things. You may be going to her place, meet the lady and mistake her to be the maid servant."

Anyway I manage to get the phone number and the address of the lady. I call immediately.

* * *

The flat in Maharaja Tagore Road is quite neatly and tastefully decorated. From a group photo hanging in the wall I come to know that the author had had his graduation from Bengal Engineering College in 1980. I have been served tea in costly bone China cup and asked to wait. The lady in question comes after some time, clad in a white sari. She is still quite bereaved. After formal introduction I come straight to the point.

"I have read all the stories in the book. Actually I have read the whole book twice. Excellent stories they are to say the least. But never ever I have read any story by him in any book or periodical. Did he use some pen name?"

I know that my question is quite meaningless. Even this author used any penname I would have remembered and recognized because of hisinimitable style. The only possibility that remains of course is Jayanta used to write only in local magazines with very limited circulations.

She answers, "I am not surprised that you have never read any of my husband's stories. They have never been published anywhere."

I have to keep the cup of tea quickly on the centre table. My hand is shaking though slightly.

"In fact I was unaware of the fact that he writes" the lady continues," he used to stay in Bhilai as he worked in the steel plant there. I teach in a government college in Kolkata so this was an arrangement we had to accept. My daughter stayed with me of course. She is now doing her PhD in IIT Kharagpur. He had a sudden stroke and passed away in office before his colleagues could even call the plant doctor. I could only attend the funeral. His employers arranged to send all his belongings to me. I found all these manuscripts in a laced file that the packers delivered. You see he was height of an introvert. Never ever did he talk of this passion to me just like he neverlet anyone know that he had some problems with the functioning of his heart."

She takes a pause probably to gather herself. How could a man create to this standard and yet keep things secret even from his nearest people, I wondered.

The review gets published in time. Following the review in our publication other reviews follow. The lady calls me and requests another visit to her place.

This day I find her much more sociable. She happily reports that the sales figures are good and are increasing. After the tea session and some small talk the lady hands me a diary.

"You didn't voice a question but you had it in your eyes the other day" said she, "you want to know why Jayanta did never make his passion known even to me. You will find the answer here. I am facing this question from many friends. Other thanme you are the first to know and you will be last to know. Please read and return it quickly." She paused and then said, "In a sense I have done something I shouldn't have done. My husband didn't want anyone to read these stories even after his death. I have made them public."

* * *

Jayanta had an affair with a lady called Anasuya right from the first year in engineering college. Actually he had to pay dearly for this affair. Anasuya had had an 'official' affair with Rajib, a close friend of Jayanta. But that affair was actually in very sorry state.

Then came that fateful monsoon day. Jayanta had gone to Anasuya's place for a light chat. Outside it was gloomy overcast day with occasional spells of rain. Anasuya was alone in the house. Suddenly they realized that they want each other. They realized that they had wanted each other badly for long and only had kept on walking on the path of self denial. Not many words were spoken, nor were they required.

In modern world people love to believe certain things as spontaneous when actually they are meticulously planned. In most cases people like to believe that he or she has fallen in love while actually these 'falling' is nothing but carefully riding a boat after weighing the pros and cons. For Jayanta and Anasuya the case was really spontaneous. Everything like social standings, relationship with other friends, commonplace taboos, inexperience were against the surrender. Yet they surrendered to each other. While it was raining without it was also raining within and just as rain washes off the dirt and gives a fresh look to nature they were feeling that they were on the verge of a new life.

As only expected all the friends shunned Jayanta. For them it was unacceptable betrayal to Rajib. Lot of stories, mostly fabricated were spread in the college circles about the capricious nature of Jayanta. Jayanta practically had to live without friends the very years of early youth when by default friends mean the world. The affair with Anasuya did last for little more than three years.

And then, one day, Anasuya ended the relationship quite casually. Just like day one it was also a gloomy day with occasional showers. Anasuya had grown what can be called an insane attraction towards celebrities and the very aspect of one becoming a celebrity. For last few months Jayanta was too tied up with final year exams and the campus interviews. So they were meeting less frequently. As Jayanta didn't have a phone in his home calling her was also not a very easy option. In this period Anasuya had befriended an artist who happened to be the nephew of a very famous artist. There was a hub in the art circles that this young man would in time prove to be the perfect torch bearer of his famous uncle. This 'sure to be celebrity' had proposed to Anasuya and Anasuya didn't take long to forget Jayanta and succumb to the proposal.

Jayanta returned home amidst the rain all soaked inside and outside. For a short period of time he did in fact contemplate committing suicide but fortunately thought better of it. But one decision he did make during that walk in the rain. He decided that he would never do anything in life which can mark him as a 'celebrity' of even a minor order.

With passage of time he discovered this passion for writing in him. Anybody who has ever felt a creative passion of any kind knows how dictatorial that passion can be. He started writing. But he checked the desire to be published or even to be read by near and dear ones so great was his disgust for the concept of fame and celebrity.

I of course go back to the lady to return the diary. By this time the collection of short stories is topping the best sellers' list. I tell her that never ever will I divulge the whole thing to anybody. (The name of the author I have used in this narrative is a changed one.)

The thing could have jolly well ended here. However, people like us attached in any way with news media are a bit too inquisitive. I thought whynot find out what Anasuya and that genius of an artist are doing today.

It proves quite easy to locate them. Anasuya today teaches in third Grade College in the suburbs.

And that genius of an artist teaches in a mediocre school as art teacher. He has tried in vain to organize exhibitions of his own work. The results were quite huge financial losses and very unfriendly reviews in few journals. He earns something extra by making some paintings for interior decorators. At times he makes paintings which adorn the walls in hotels.

There is no signature at the corners of those paintings as they he has got no signature value.

Status-quo

Right now I am waiting with Samiran in the shabby reception area of a cheap nursing home. There is sufficient reason to be worried and worried we are. When we tried to get some reassurance from the doctor and the nurses all we could get mechanical replies like, 'Please wait outside, we are trying our best.'

According to the foils found Parna has consumed seventy six sleeping pills. Nobody can say for sure when she did this. Her husband understood what has happened at around nine in the morning. Her husband Samiran is my neighbour from childhood days. He opted for this non-descript nursing home as he feared going to some place of repute would immediately attract the attention of law. None of us could make Samiran understand the dangers of going for this ill equipped nursing home with such critical a patient.

The fact that Samiran and Parna's marriage was not working well is an open secret. In fact things had been so almost since the beginning. They are childless. Parna used to teach in a local primary school. She had had to give up the job upon Samiran's relentless insistence. Samiran did suspect that Parna was developing some sort of attraction towards the young clerk of the school. Needless to say there was no truth in the suspicions but people like Samiran who are not man enough love to nurture such thoughts. They even take pride in taking the 'right action' driven by these filthy ideas. This 'right action' no doubt contributed in deteriorating their relationship.

Dr. Ghosal, the senior doctor of the house, comes out. Samiran and I spring from our seats and stand questioningly in front of him. He looks at me with sufficient indignation, goes to the corner of the veranda spits out the beetle leaf that he was chewing and says, "I cannot say anything now. We are trying and that's all." Parna had taken the sleeping pills in the bath and when the door was broken she was found asleep in the floor of the bath.

There is a background story of Dr. Ghosal's annoyance at my presence. The incident happened about an year or so back. A middle class couple who already had a kid went to Dr. Ghosal for abortion. Dr. Ghosal did the job so well that the lady died. In such cases the normal aftermath would have been jail term for Dr. Ghosal and stripping of his registration as medical practitioner. Samiran, myself and others of the locality wanted and expected these things to happen.

Samiran works as a clerk in Kolkata police headquarters. So Dr. Ghosal was particularly afraid of him after the mishap. Just two days after the incident I returned from office and my mother reported that Birenda, the local committee secretary of the ruling party had visited our home and had requested me to attend a meeting in the party office at seven in the evening that very day. Samiran called and said that

Birenda had visited his home as well and had left the same request.

Anyway we reached the party office few minutes before the scheduled time. Among others present we found Dr. Ghosal. Dr. Ghosal was an active party worker so we were not exactly surprised to find him there. We asked others about the agenda of the meeting but none could say anything explicitly. The surprise came when the meeting started. The single agenda of the meeting was the lady's death.

Presently Yadav, the husband of the hapless lady joined the meeting. Yadav worked as an orderly in the local municipality office, a job he had bagged with the help of Birenda. After beating about the bush for some time I heard Birenda saying, "....to err is human. Sushanta (Dr. Ghosal) had tried his best. We did conduct an enquiry on behalf of our party and we are convinced about it. We all know the result of an operation always does not depend on the surgeon alone. Life and death are at times beyond the control of mere mortals and we have to accept it. We have also decided that henceforth all costs of studies of Yadav's daughter will be borne by the Party. I would therefore like to request Yadav to withdraw his allegations against Dr. Ghosal and request everybody of the locality to consider the case closed. Talking acrimoniously about the incident will not help anyone."

Now it was clear why Samiran and I had been called. I was known in the locality as sort of maverick character and because of my job in enforcement directorate I was well acquainted with people in important positions. And Samiran worked in the police headquarters of Kolkata. So

Birenda understood and quite correctly that it was necessary to keep us bridled else we could prove to be difficult for Dr. Ghosal. Not that we were convinced in the meeting but we had to keep tongue tied for the interest of Yadav and his daughter. The very next day Yadav came to my home to report something that was not discussed in the meeting. Yadav had been 'informed' by an aide of Birenda that he had practically no option, either he would have to withdraw the FIR or he would lose his job in the municipality. Needless to say that Yadav withdrew his complaint made to the police. The thing is now past but Dr. Ghosal has not forgotten that Samiran and I had wanted to put him behind the bars.

By now we have made another unsuccessful attempt at peeking inside. They have said the very same thing, 'Efforts are on, please wait." How long does it take to pump the stomach of a person?

Samiran's father is a regular taker of these sleeping pills. He is a patient of chronic depression and this has been going on for years now. I believe that never ever had he been treated properly by any good psychiatrist. Some general physicians work as covert psychiatrists and some such semi quack has 'treated' him all along. Unfortunately even in this day some people have got sky high taboo about going to psychiatrists and that's the opportunity these people grab to make quick bucks. Parna has used his father in law's prescription to purchase the sleeping pills. But the point is no chemist is supposed to sell so many foils of sedative against one prescription at a time. So has she taken a long time to create her bank of sedatives? Was she planning this for long? If she doesn't recover these questionswill remain unanswered. The biggest chemist shop in this locality is "Ma Tara Pharmacy". For long I have been receiving various complaints against them. It was reported that they sell drugs without prescriptions and also their paperwork are not always in order. If it is proven that they have sold all the foils together I will not let go this opportunity to screw them. But it all depends on what happens to Parna.

Honestly speaking many a time I have feared that Parna may do something desperate like this. Actually I knew her and her conditions too well to fear all these. She is sensitive, highly emotional and the least calculative a person can be. And that's precisely why I find the proposition of planned buying of sleeping pills in various instalments so absurd.

She used to come to my father for taking tuitions in mathematics. I am about four years senior to her. I still remember on the days she was there I used to visit my father's study much more frequently than normal. Normally father used to teach her along with two other girls but my I was not a bit interested in others and always I tried to show that I am least interested in her as well. At that time she was a student of class VIII and I was in class XII. Young ladies are born with much stronger radar than young men can imagine and one day she made no bones of the fact that she was well aware of my interest in her. That day she was alone as other students were absent and my father had gone out for some time. It was raining heavily. As usual I had visited the room on the pretext of an exercise book I had ostensibly left there, when she suddenly lifted her head from and said me something that left me startled and thrilled me beyond description.

She said, "Come and have a seat here. Even a child can see through your pretence. You are looking for something in the same place for ten times." I was left with only one alternative of giving a sheepish smile and accept her invitation and that's precisely what I did. We had a nice time chatting together as blissfully father came back quite late. However, that semi romantic meeting had had no follow ups.

I was really good in studies. Did my honours in Chemistry from Presidency College and went to IISC Bangalore for my masters. Once, while I was back in home in a vacation came to know that Parna and Samiran were going to tie the knot very soon. At times I had seen them roaming around together and though I did not exactly cherish the news it didn't come to me as a surprise. I did cut short my vacation on the pretext of some project work and went back to Bangalore simply because I didn't want to honour the invitation to the marriage party.

Suddenly I am jerked out of my reverie as I find Birenda has arrived with a few of his party comrades. Since the incident of Yadav's wife I generally avoid him. But now I felt that he is needed here. He can get the actual information about what is happening inside. Birenda casually pushes the swing door and goes inside. In fact he enjoys this sort of access in any house and establishment of the locality. By this time Samiran has pinched three cigarettes from my packet, now he picks up the fourth one lights it and says, "Amu I think things have turned for the worse. Maybe she is no more. I am only a petty clerk but you are well placed. Please see that the matter doesn't go to the police."

I somehow contain my immediate impulse of giving him a tight slap. I knew that he is dense but could not fathom how much insensitive a man can be when is wife is either dying or already dead. Then I observe Birenda and Dr. Ghosal coming out of the main swing door. I move a few paces towards them with Samiran close in my heels. The pumping operation has failed so to say. The particular type of sleeping pills consumed by Parna is of a fast dissolve formulation. Parna is still alive but in deep sleep similar to coma. That means now it is only a question of time and she will breathe her last in sleep. I look at Samiran. He seems more bothered about how to keep the death from police than bereaved at the imminent loss. I feel that I am looking at a murderer.

I find no reason to be there anymore. Waiting here for the news of Parna's death seemed too vulture like. I reach home, take a shower, announce lack of appetite and retire to my bed. It is about one PM in the afternoon. Most likely the cremation will be tomorrow after autopsy and all. Samiran will not feel an iota of grief, instead Parna will be blamed for all the trouble she has put Samiran into. What is the meaning of such marriages?

*   *   *

Parna has not realized that I have entered her room. Seeing that she is not there I decide that she must have gone out and will be returning shortly. So I settle in an easy chair and start leafing through a magazine. I hear a noise of latch and the door to the washroom opens and Parna comes out. She was in the shower. She is still drying her hair with a short towel.

She is stark naked. Absent minded as she is she has completely forgotten that she did leave the door to her bedroom ajar. She is oblivious to my presence and is humming a tune. I am looking at her agape completely incapable of take my eyes off though I know it is purely unethical. Her beautiful fair back is adorned by her hair and there is a red mole at the back of her left shoulder. It is a cloudy day and just at this moment the rain starts. Parna suddenly notices me and with a short cry pulls a sari from the stand. By now I am standing just in front of her completely mesmerized. She is hardly covered in the sari she has drawn. Just at this moment Samiran enters smoking a cigarette. He is not at all astonished in seeing his wife standing naked in front of another man and says casually, "Hallo...so you are here, let me share good news, Parna is pregnant. I know you have lots of friends in medical circle. Please arrange some discount for your poor friend." Samiran goes out and at that moment my phone rings.

I am jerked out of sleep. What a dream! The phone is ringing still. But before I come fully to my senses and locate the phone, the ring ceases. Its dusk now and my room is almost dark. Somehow I manage to switch on a light and grab my phone. I find four missed calls from Samiran. Why the creep is in such hurry to break the bad news? I ring up Samiran.

- Yes when did she pass away?
- No Amu, she is fine, completely out of danger

- But how is that possible after seventy six sleeping pills?
- You better come over.

Samiran hangs up.

I find both Samiran and Birenda waiting for me at the nursing home gate. Before I can ask anything I am whisked away to a nearby small dingy room and Birenda closes the door. Then he says, "Amu, nobody should speak a single word. Parna is saved because all the pills she had consumed were counterfeit. But if you sing a lot of people will be in trouble. So you have to give me your word." Birenda lights a cigarette in leisure waiting for my answer.

I am back home now. I can forever shut down that pharmacy and send the owner to jail by a simple report. But then I will have to disclose the fact that Parna had attempted suicide. I can also reopen the case of Yadav's wife and bring that Dr. Ghosal to book. Strictly speaking the revelation to law that Parna had attempted suicide is not my problem. But still I know that I have to keep my mouth shut.

Because by this time Dr. Ghosal knows that Parna is pregnant. He is also armed with the knowledge that Samiran is biologically incapable of becoming a father. It is neither difficult for him to understand who the father of the child is nor will it be possible to suppress the fact that Parna was driven to taking the ultimate step because of me. And if Samiran refuses to take the child it is the same Dr. Ghosal who will be required for carrying out the abortion.

Next day being a Sunday I wake up late. My elder brother's son Biltu loves playing in my room. When I wake up I find Biltu making castle with playing cards. The castle is three stories high.

Suddenly the castle of cards seem very symbolic to me. A little light stroke can bring the castle down. But nobody will be fool enough to do so and that's how status quo of the civilized society is maintained.

The Reality Show

Damayanti is a runner. You will find her if you stay in Sonarpur and got a habit of taking a stroll in early morning. A slim figure in a cheap pair of Cades, hair tucked in ponytail, a faded discoloured tracksuit- running along the road is a regular sight in early mornings. The tracksuit is a mark of charity received from another athlete who could afford to throw away the old set. Damayanti is quite a figure in local circles and people, even the cynical elders have some sort of respect for this devoted lady. By this time Damayanti has won the district championships for two consecutive years.

Damayanti's father Ajit works as foreman in Arvind Fusion Company. Ajit is proud of her daughter at the same time Damayanti's passion makes him sad. He knows Damayanti cannot carry it too far. It takes money to pursue the dream of being an athlete. He has not earned his wages for last three months.

One day, almost unknown to himself Ajit had entered the blind alley of trade unionism. That day Tapan, a fellow worker was working with an old electric rotary saw and another worker Paran was working in the milling machine a short distance away. Suddenly the saw went off the handle and whirled towards Paran. Tapan could only cry out and

Paran could move only a few inches. Otherwise he would have lost his life. But he did indeed lose his life in a different sense. The circular saw spinning at high speed hit his right wrist and his right hand dropped on the ground severed from the wrist. Immediately Paran was carried off to the nearby government hospital by his comrades. Aslam, another worker, even carried the severed hand. Probably he had thought that doctors in that hospital are endowed with superhuman qualities and can stitch back the hand to the wrist!

Paran's life could be saved but not his job. Who has ever heard of a machinist deprived of his most precious possession, the right hand? A trade union tried to fight with the management for proper compensation. Incidentally Paran was close friend of Ajit so he got involved in the movement forParan's compensation. A deputation of workers was presented in the office of the general manager of the company. Ajit did lead the deputation and he was the main speaker. It was put forward that the management had been warned time and again that the tools were not in workable condition. Working with them was not safe. All these words had fallen to deaf ears time and again.

The general manager did silently hear all the allegations against the management and at the end offered compensations which were meagre even by the highest of hyperbole possible. Ajit could remain sober any longer and left the room after showering volley of acrimonious words. To his extreme dismay he observed a few days later Paran leaving the factory for the last time with tears in his eyes. He had had accepted the little whatever was offered as 'compensation' and the trade union people were conspicuous by absence from the scene.

Little did Ajit know that in this ugly world of give and take things do not move in a straight line. He did however shun all connections with the trade union. This incident was closely followed by retrenchment of some of the workers, including Ajit. No trade union made it a cause for movement. It was three months back.

In these three months Ajit has done lot of odd jobs including (but not limited to) ferrying toffees in the bus and trams, delivering letters and parcels for a small courier company, working as housekeeping staff in a petty hotel but none of these has given any sustained support. Now he is planning to open a small shop for selling cigarettes and a sort of chewable concoction made from beetle leaves. In this land where number of factories shut down every day getting a job in a factory is exercise of utopia of highest order.

Ajit finds a great friend in Damayanti. When Ajit's wife tirelessly showers harsh words on Ajit for his lack of common sense, which she does quite often, Damayanti feels pained. Late at night when her mother and brother are fast asleep Damayanti sits with his father near the open door of their hut andthe two have a sweet time. The city is quiet and doesn't seem to be harsh. Ajit speaks of his various experiences and many anecdotes and Damayanti talks of her dreams, how she has been able to clock better time and where she will reach one day. A sweet breeze that cools off the city soothes them as well. At times Damayanti sings a song for her father. Not that she is a great singer, neither she has a good stock of lyrics but still they enjoy the time like anything. Even the moon seems to come down as if to eagerly listen to their chat.

Her studies have ended after she passed plus two level of school. She was not at all interested in going for graduation. Ajit had had dreams that Damayanti will become a graduate one day but Damayanti's own dreams are different. And practical minded as she is she understood that given the meagre resources Ajit could spare, pursuing both athletics and education was not possible.

When Damayanti goes for a run alone, she runs on and on, she feels she is in a different world. This world does not know any poverty, any incompleteness, somewhat like the world a child dreams of. She has won the district championships for two consecutive years. The local councillor has given word that he will get her a job in the municipality. Recently she has taken the job of games teacher in a small privately run school. The salary is nothing to boast of but still when at the end of the month she manages to give some money to her father the feeling for both is priceless. Ajit feels that in this rude unfriendly world where needs always far outgrow capacity, he is after all not alone, he has someone to hold his hand.

Damayanti loves watching sports shows in the television. Ajit did manage to get an old television set that changes colour of its own will and often becomes black and white. The local cable TV operator does not charge Ajit for the connection he has provided. This is his tribute to Damayanti who after all is a celebrity in the local circles. Recently number of channels has started daring 'reality shows'. Such shows are must watch for Damayanti.

Rekha, Ajit's wife is suffering with multiple complaints these days. The municipality doctor had advised some investigations and Ajit has got them done with considerable difficulty. Today he had gone to the hospital to show the reports and has come back quite devastated.

There is a tumour in her stomach and Rekha needs immediate surgery. The cost of the surgery is actually quite prohibitive for a man like Ajit. Ajit starts running to the councillors and political leaders. A recommendation can fetch big discounts in the surgery costs.

In the morning Damayanti says that she is going to Kolkata, the nearby big city and won't be back before evening.

"What about your classes in the school?" asks Ajit.

"I have taken a day off" says Damayanti and starts to go out. Her job as games teacher, which very much depends upon the frills and fancies of the owner, is right now only steady income of the household. Naturally Ajit feels a bit uneasy but refrains from saying anything.

* * *

A month has passed. Right now Damayanti is in Mumbai. Actually she had gone to Kolkata to appear for the audition of a reality show. She has passed and now she is in Mumbai for the shoot. Like all other reality shows the hosts of this show makes the performers perform daring acts. At times they have to put their hand in a bowl full of scorpions or walk along the edge of the roof of a twenty storied high building. Of course safety precautions are there but still they are quite challenging and can turn dangerous. Thrill sells at a premium and so the shows have got high popularity ratings and are aired in prime time. Ajit of course didn't know all these. Damayanti had said she had got a well-paid job that required her to relocate to Mumbai. Not that Ajit was exactly happy to let Damayanti leave for Mumbai but what choice did he have? The world is run by financial needs and not by love and wishes. Rekha's surgical operation was pending, (in fact is pending still), new year was approachingrequiring quite a good amount of money to buy books and session fees for Damayanti's brother. Damayanti did comfort him saying this being a much better job she would be able to send money to solve all these needs.

Ajit did get a jolt for life time about ten days later. It was an ordinary evening and like all other evenings Ajit was seated in the tea stall near his home. These tea stalls are sort of meeting ground for the common folk. With simple idle gossip with topics ranging from local scandals to national politics these become peoples' parliaments. Also news of prospective new jobs or short term assignments are received here.

That day when Ajit was planning to leave the shop a local urchin Baptu came running and said, "Uncle you are seated here, they are showing acts of Damayanti in TV, go and see...Du Plus Channel". Ajit wanted to know more but by then Baptu was gone. Ajit ran home and turned on the TV.

A square frame of iron rods with each side about twenty metres in length was hanging at a height of about a ten storied building. Damayanti was walking on that frame and moving from one corner to the other. Damayanti's brother is quite smart. He said, "This is not a live show. I think it was recorded few days back." Ajit could take it no longer. He immediately called Damayanti and shouted, "If this is your job, to hell with your job! Come back to Kolkata now." He was beside himself with tension. Damayanti was sleeping after a gruelling day of shooting. She sleepily said, "Don't worry; there is always a safety belt. I have shot one episode today and only one is left. Then I will be coming to Kolkata, bye." She hung up.

Ajit could not have his dinner that night. A deep sense of guilt and anger towards his own destiny was eating into him. The anger was of course totally impotent and he knew that himself. There was no way denying that he had failed miserably in his duties as a family man. He had seen in the streets some gypsy sort of people making their children perform dangerous sort of acts just for a few pennies. Seeing them do such things with theirchildren he had used harsh words to describe their means of making a living. "Today", he sadly thought, "I am making my loving daughter do thousand times more dirty work as I can't earn enough". There are some fires that can never be doused. They burn within and keep on making the person charred.

Damayanti is now a hero and her fame has spread much beyond the local circles. She and only other participant have been able to reach the final rounds of the show. Her picture now adorns the billboards put in all major cities. Often Ajit is stopped in the road and congratulated by gentlemen who erstwhile never bothered to recognize him. Ajit thanks them but can never do so from heart. How can he tell others that because of the fun of the nation he is spending sleepless nights?

Unlike other episodes the final episode is being telecast live. The contestant is to stand on the edge of a building twenty stories high. Some two metres away from her a net is hanging in an iron frame. She has to jump and catch the net and then slowly the net will be brought down to the ground. But meanwhile the contestant has to crawl along the net and reach a particular area on the net. And to add to the charm no safety belt has been provided to the contestants!

The only other contestant is Suman a lady from Punjab. She makes three attempts and fails. The producer of the show calls Damayanti aside and says that she has to make it and increases her fees on the spot.

Damayanti comes to the edge, concentrates; she cannot afford to make any mistake. Three faces flashed through her mind and she realized that she is now calm and has got complete command on herself and she leaps and lands neatly on the net, clasping the net.

But what the hell! As soon as she caught the net with two hands one side of the net gave away from the frame. So practically her load is now on one hand. Far below on the ground another net has been placed to prevent extreme fatality if some contestant loses nerve midway. If someone had toldher that a contestant can think in such a condition she would have discarded that as absurd, but now actually Damayanti is thinking.

She is thinking if she falls or fails to complete the show properly her brother's schooling will stop, her father's shop will never see the light of the day and she will be begging on the street as a cripple.

She is feeling like her arm will tear off. Tears are rolling down her cheeks. But she pulls herself together and starts moving toward the spot of the net where she has to go. By now as per the plan the net should start descending but it has not started.

She is also feeling that the frame is being mechanically shaken to make her work even more difficult. Suddenly like a flash it becomes clear to her. The net has not come off on one side by accident. It was a plan made to add to the thrill of the spectators! So also the frame is being shaken and is not being brought down as planned.

Damayanti feels a burst of rage within her. She feels that if she can alight safe and sound she will give a strong kick at the balls of the producer. And strangely this rage gives her the strength she so badly needed at this hour. She crawls along the net to reach the spot and now she realizes that the net is descending.

Damayanti's mother can't watch the show any more, she is now praying to God. Ajit has bitten his lip in tension and is now bleeding. A projection TV has been arranged in the tea stall and all the men and women have gathered in front of it to watch the show. The tea stall vendor has record sale today.

Suddenly Damayanti's head reels as she had looked down and it seemed she would fall. A huge cry arose from all watching the show in the street. But, thank heavens, she recovers and resumes the crawl. A commentator is giving running commentary of the proceedings with his arsenal full of exciting words.

Damayanti now knows she can do it but is still not certain. She is not thinking of any God. In fact she is thinking nothing now, only three faces, of her mother, brother and father are flashing in her mind in turn.

The producer of the show is busy taking calls from various corporate houses who want to book a slot in the next performance of Damayanti. Of course the calls are being filtered by his secretary and only the first ranking corporate are allowed reaching him. Three internationally renowned media broadcasting companies and five leading newspapers have also called meanwhile.

Damayanti has reached the designated spot. A huge uproar can be heard from people who gathered at the spot to see the action live. (Unlike other days recordings of uproar are not used or required today). Slowly the frame is brought down to ground.

Two doctors and paramedics run to assist her. She holds the hand of a lady paramedic and steadies herself, takes a little water and waves to the people. A deafening uproar is heard which is joined by many such uproars around the country including one in the tea stall show. Ajit opened his eyes and gave cry of joy. Last few minutes he was sitting with his eyes tightly shut.

The Producer comes towards Damayanti with a wide grin and a cheque in his hand. Damayanti has a momentary impulse to give him the kick he deserves so heavily and divulge the nasty plan of making the show more thrilling to the reporters gathered and so eager to talk to her. But she does nothing of the sort.

She accepts the hug of the uncouthly overweight producer, accepts the cheque and smiles to the crowd and camera.

* * *

Coming out of the airport Damayanti finds Ajit standing with his son. She rushes to the arms of her father. For a second tears glisten in her eyes and then she says "You can talk to the surgeon and fix up the date for mother's surgery now, and also we will plan your shop together and start buying things. I want to see you shop start before I leave."

- You will have to go again?
- This is a job papa. I can't say no. Don't worry these things are much easier abroad.
- Abroad?
- Yes the next round of shoot is in Johannesburg, South Africa.

The Demon's Tale

Susmit is suffering kaleidoscope of disquieting thoughts inside his head for quite some time now. He has tried everything that he thought would help. Nothing has helped. Some of the thoughts he has suffered in the past hour are actually quite nihilistic in nature. Like he had thought of jumping from the balcony of his apartment which is actually in the seventh floor and the thought had brought a short lived sense of relief. In fact he has stood up and had started walking towards the balcony when sense dawned upon him and he slumped back in his couch where he had been sitting for past three hours.

The phone is ringing. Even though it is not any special ring tone Susmit can say that Gopa is calling. Susmit let the phone have its whole ring and then it stops. What's the use in taking the call from Gopa? She will say the very same things, the same sorry tone of despair will drive Susmit one more step towards a bottomless abyss as he knows there is no way he can help the situation.

Like all other boys Susmit used to play soccer in his teens. Once, he suddenly remembered, a bully sort of a boy had made a powerful kick which did land in his shin bone and the effect was a claustrophobic sense of acute pain. Susmit did feel like he was covered in a glass jar from where he could see everybody but hear none and this jar was made of sense of pain. If he could come out he could get rid of the pain as well. Today's situation is somewhat similar to that painful captivity of years back. The whole thing has started yesterday and that too quite suddenly.

Susmit stays alone in this apartment and Gopa comes at times. They are slated to get married in coming December. Since it's the just two of them in the whole apartment traditional Indian values normally are thrown to winds and they spend the time in seventh heaven of happiness. However Gopa never spends nights here. Gopa's father cannot so easily digest the idea of premarital intimacy.One day after making love Susmitcasually picked up his Nikon and started clicking pictures of his beau. A great advantage of the digital age is complete privacy is so easily assured.

At first Gopa was quite bashful about being photographed nude. She pulled a sheet and covered herself. Thousand requests of Susmit had no positive effect. However after a few days, in a similar situation she herself started taking pictures and since then Susmit has taken hundreds of intimate photographs. Later on Susmit transfer the photographs to his desktop and he enjoys them in solitude. Susmit loves looking at the nude pictures of his lady love taken from various angles and in different postures. They fill Susmit with an inexplicable sense of happiness.

He has realized that contrary to popular notion, the real use of the contraption for taking photographs is not for recording hitherto unseen or unknown subjects. Rather much greater use of camera is in photographing known people. Camera sees many things that are hardly observed in normal vision. Gopa has long hair. But before photographing her like this he had never observed her long hair on her bare back looks so heavenly. Or for that matter he had never noticed her nude, plus size reclining figure looks like as if waves of an ocean have suddenly frozen to create a female form!

-       Do you like taking same snaps every day?
        You are really strange.

One day Gopa had said. Susmit didn't try to explain. Everything cannot be explained and all pleasures cannot be shared. Susmit stores the pictures in a particular directory of his computer which is password protected. Normally there is no visitor in this flat except Gopa, the maid and occasionally Susmit's parents who come from their native small town some two hundred miles from Kolkata. So much of caution is therefore more than necessary, but Susmit is like that. May be he is also not completely free of taboo regarding his intimacy and so he overtly secretive.

Once he was generous and tried to show his 'collection' to Gopa. Gopa did enjoy for some time but then suddenly she got engulfed in an avalanche of shame and the pictures seemed too profane and she insisted to stop the show.

On that fateful Sunday Gopa had come in early. Her parents had gone on an outing and she tried to make best use of the time. After spending some time together both of them felt they should go for a drive in the newly procured car of Susmit. They drove for some time along a state high way and then took a turn and entered an unnamed avenue. The road was picturesque with paddy fields and trees on both sides. The sky was overcast that gave the scene an effect found in Constable's paintings. At this point to add to the drama the perfectionist Gentleman turned on rain. And what a shower it was with maddening smell of earth when it gets drenched by the first rain!

After a while their self-restraint gave away and they stopped the car and went out to get drenched. Little did they care to lock the car when they went out! Actually why should they have cared? There was nobody visible anywhere. When they were getting drenched Gopa cried out, 'See there is no one else, we are the first man and the first woman in the world'.

On their way back Gopa first noticed the loss. Susmit used to keep his Nikon in a small cloth bag and the bag with the Nikon was missing from the back seat where it was kept. Actually the trance of getting drenched was still continuing else they would have spotted it earlier. The breeze on their soaked clothing in the moving car was creating sort of intoxication. There was no point in going back now so they accepted the loss and drove home.

* * *

Susmit had had a sort of sketchy idea about office politics, fight of gladiators blinded by jealousy etc. but he could not imagine the snake basket like condition that exists in reality. In fact rivalry is not unknown in the formative steps of school and college but there the big advantage is use ofmasks is not mandatory. A few years after joining his first job Susmit did see a public notice in office about dress code which read that the office code was 'smart casuals', jeans and t shirts were allowed only on Fridays, but no polo neck or snickers etc. and etc. He gave a wry smile and told his boss, "They have written everything but have missed out the very important item that we have to put on every day and every minute". His boss obviously failed to grasp the meaning and but since that he could not afford to divulge he gave an idiotic laugh of 'appreciation'.

Attendingparties thrown by detestable colleagues is a mandatory torment for sensitive souls. Today Susmit was feeling a growing sense of restlessness in Mukherjee's house. He had come with Gopa to attend one of such tormenting parties. Mukherjee's would be father in law has presented him with an apartment where he would be living with his would be wife Kasturi. The apartment is fully furnished. The party was arranged in this apartment. The guests comprised of five couples and would be couples who are similar in rank with Mukherjee. The colonial rulers may have left the land about seventy years ago but they have left behind some loyalists like Mukherjee who staunchly believe in colonial values. So Mukherjee always maintain a visible distance with people who are working in lower grades. For people in upper grades of course his attitude takes a somersault.

Gopa did want to avoid but unfortunately it was discovered that Kasturi, Mukherjee's would be wife, was her batch mate in the same college and so escape routes were practically closed. After a few pegs the discussions turned quite 'bold' with erotic jokes and the like. Mukherjee drove the discussion to the topic of porn and cyber porn. Generally men are more knowledgeable in such matters than women.

After some time Mukherjee turned on his computer and started exhibiting his collection of downloaded porn photos.

There was a mild murmur of protest from the ladies but other than Gopa's the protest of others were cosmetic and Gopa was too sober to make hisprotest loud, so the slide show continued. After a few slides came the devastating slides. Gopa and Susmit felt weak in the knee.

They were complete nude photos of Gopa and Susmit taken in Susmit's apartment. A dodge of colour did cover the faces of both but who needs to see his or her own face to recognize own photos? With herculean effort they managed to keep straight face. Susmit understood that someone has recognized them and that is Mukherjee himself, the host of the ghastly show. The thief who stole the camera must have sold it somewhere and either he himself or his buyer has posted the photos in some pornographic site. By a ruthless turn of fate Mukherjee has spotted the photos, downloaded them and has covered the faces with paint in Photoshop specifically for the public show. And for making the show Mukherjee has plan fully steered the discussion towards porn. In fact the entire party was organized for that purpose.

That the covering of faces has been done by Mukherjee is also unmistakably proved by another fact. The company logo on the jacket thrown casually at the back of the chair, as visible in the photo, is also covered by paint. No casual porn lover in the world would have cared to do it.

Mukherjee closed the show just after showing the photos of Susmit and Gopa. This was also not by accident. Susmit knows why Mukherjee did it. After watching a movie the audience comes out with the last scenes in mind. So Mukherjee chose to end the 'movie' at that point. Eating at this mental state was no less than third degree torture, but they had to eat something. Susmit dropped Gopa at her home and then returned to his apartment.

It was half past nine when he had returned and now it is 02 AM. Susmit is still seated in his couch. Gopa had called twice. First time she could hardly talk and sobbed and sobbed. In her next call she managed to talk though quite incoherently. They discussed what further damage Mukherjee may cause to them with the nude photographs. Susmit had had an impulse of thrashing Mukherjee'sheadwith some blunt instrument but has somehow managed to forget such nonsense.

Susmit is awakened by the calling bell of his maid servant. He has spent the night in the couch and had actually dozed off when it was near dawn. The cool breeze and the soft glow of dawn makes even troubled minds surrender to sleep. He takes a cup of tea and goes for shower. The cool water helps to get the thoughts organized. He decides that he must catch hold of the culprit who has posted the photos in the net. There must be some way to track down the man. There is a cybercrime branch in city police headquarters where he must go today. I have got to bunk office.

*   *   *

Susmit had no idea that a routine fortnightly meeting in his office can turn out like this. This meeting is the common meeting ground of managers of all projects with the Project Director. Mukherjee and Susmit manage separate set of projects with totally different teams and so chances of their roads crossing each other's' is quite low. But there are certain policy matters that affect all.

In recent days the management is trying to take some unpopular measures on the pretext of business being slow. Today's meeting was basically for getting the consent of the project managers for implementing these measures. Even the office cupboards know that Mukherjee is a shameless 'yes man' of the management. But today he outdid all his past performances. Actually his game plan was clear. He had surmised while everybody will be opposing such damaging moves he would stand apart and support the management and thereby curries favour during the yearly appraisals. Flattery is a trap where all people walk in with pleasure more or less. Some bossedin fact rush into such snares. Mukherjee uses this nature of bosses to a tee and nobody has forgotten in last office party he practically worked as waiter for the table of top bosses. Everybody try to ignore this nuisance of office as trouble they have to live with. But today, when Mukherjee was justifying the proposals of management with self devised logics even new tothe perpetrators of the proposals, Susmit could not display such philosopher like aloofness anymore and blurted out, "You also know what is being done is not correct but you are doing all these only to appease the bosses!" Suddenly silence fell on the room like a drop scene in an ill managed amateur theatre. The Executive Director finishes the meeting and summons Susmit to his chamber.

When Susmit had visited the cybercrime cell of police in the police headquarters he had had better expectations. He had thought that though these people are police all the same since they deal with a specialized and sophisticated type of crime some sophistication could be expected from them as well. They would at least realize the feeling of distress natural when one sees nude photos of his lady love are making rounds in porn circuits. At first the officer (but probably not a gentleman) who met Susmit and heard the case tried to shake it off as a case of simple theft and hence not in the purview of cybercrime. Susmit had to explain the situation in detail again and now the man gave a long draw at the cigarette he was smoking and said, "So your girlfriend was completely naked. How interesting! I knew only porn stars give such shots." Susmit was feeling nauseated. The man continued, "So have you brought sample of photos that you have lost?"

Susmit was prepared for this question; he silently handed over the pen drive where some similar shots were stored. They can be called similar because they were taken in the same location and in same state but on some other day. The man eagerly inserted the pen drive in his desk top computer; quickly opened the folder viewed a few snaps and then snapped at Susmit, "What is this! You have covered the faces with paint. If you camouflage like this how do you expect we can find out from which IP address these photos were posted?"

Susmit did put up a feeble resistance, "Why?Can't you recognize the photo from the surroundings? The photos posted in the net were taken in the same room."

The officer now reclined in his seat, lighted another cigarette and said, "Listen Mr. Adhikary, probably you have no idea that we receive suchcomplaints every day and the count is few hundred over a week. So called lovers are sleeping with their girls, taking stills and videos and posting them in net. Do you know how many pornographic sites are doing business based on supply solely from this city? And these men, sorry lovers, are handsomely paid for their merchandise."

Susmit somehow suppressed the growing inclination of thrashing the head of the officer with the computer monitor and said, "But in our case it is totally different."

"That's the beauty of the whole matter," said the officer "when we get complaints from the girls and nab the 'lovers' they also say the same thing, that their cameras or mobile phones have been stolen and they have no idea who posted these photos in the net. See man, since you have come with a reference I am explaining all these to you. Otherwise we do not spend time like these. You need to realize it is like finding a needle in hay stack. Do you know seventy percent of all websites around the world are basically porn sites? And everyday millions of such photos of naked women are being uploaded in all such sites. Try to imagine how difficult it is to spot the source of a particular photo. And you are telling me to spot it looking at the surroundings! Bring complete unedited photos; let us see what we can do."

Susmit understood that he was dismissed and got up. A relative of Gopa is a retired police officer who was in a high rank in this office and that was the 'reference'. Gopa of course didn't divulge everything to him; he was only told that Susmit was facing a problem related to cybercrime.

The statesmen also make big mistakes. Later on term them as 'Himalayan blunder'. Susmit is no statesman; he is a common man with no special act of courage to boast of. Somewhere at the back parlour of his brain probably he had a sense of guilt because of this premarital relation with Gopa. That sense of guilt has now become very biting after the act was publicized. He should have understood after the meeting with the police officer that he should drop the idea altogether of taking recourse to law. But Susmit, disturbed as he was, failed to take a lesson.

Actually things were happening that added to the distress of Susmit every day. The day after Susmit's visit to the cybercrime cell his office colleague Souvik suddenly called upon him and asked, "Where from have you bought the sofa set in your flat Susmit? They are just splendid. And the carpet I think is imported isn't it so?"

Souvik has never ever stepped into the apartment where Susmit lives. He is sort of soul mate of Mukherjee. That means Mukherjee has already started making the photos public.

As per appointment Susmit arrives at the apartment of the relative of Gopa who was a big shot in the police headquarters. The gentleman is a widower. His only son is settled with his family in Texas. This gentleman gives a patient hearing to the whole matter. Then fills and lights his pipe. Then he asks Susmit to wait and retires to the adjoining room. From the noise made by the telephone set Susmit understands that the gentleman is dialling someone from the extension kept in the bedroom. Susmit does something which is unethical by all means but he can't help doing in his present state of mind. He tiptoes to the door of the room from where the call is being made. The door is drawn but not tightly shut so Susmit can hear with some difficulty the conversation that followed.

What Susmit hears is something like this, "Halo Mr. Mallick, I am Ghosh...remember me? A young man has recently met you with my reference....yes yes Susmit...yes he took some naked photos of his girlfriend and now is in soup...you think it is a hopeless case? Yes I think so too... at most the local police can catch the guy who stole the camera...Ok I will see that the particular police station gets a special instruction...thanks buddy...buy..."

The gentleman comes back to his sit and lights his pipe again. He is actually some sort of distant uncle of Gopa. Susmit of course had resumed his position in time. The retired officer puffs at his pipe and says, "I just had a talk with a very important man. We will nab the culprit, don't worry. Not a very big deal. You do something. Give me the unedited photos. You may send to my email as well. Don't be ashamed. We are like doctors...curing the diseases of the society. And you know doctors got to be told everything. Okay?"

The uncle sees off Susmit from the gate. When he is entering his car he says, "But one thing, I believe it is better to be discreet. Don't tell Gopa that I am investigating the matter or I have seen the photographs. After all she is my relative and I don't love complications. And also women are hardly rational...you know."

In Susmit's office there is a tea boy who serves tea twice a day. Susmit remembers seeing Pradip approaching with tray full of tea cups and nothing else. Because at that point he had crashed to the floor with his chair and went to complete blackout. He regains consciousness in sick room of the office with a doctor by his side. Doctor says that his blood pressure is quite high, he must immediately go home and have complete rest for a few days.

Susmit is now walking along the road and suddenly there is a gush of wind. How strange! The weather was sultry till a few minutes back and so where from has this gush of wind come? But he could not think of the wind as to his utter dismay he realize that the wind has taken away his tee-shirt. How can a wind take away a well stitched and well-fitting tee-shirt! And then there was another gush and this time his Bermudais gone and he is left only in his boxers! What the hell is happening! The wind is affecting nobody else like this. In fact everybody else in the street has stopped and is laughing at him. Susmit is out for his morning stroll and little did he predict such ordeal. What happens if another gush of wind comes and makes him naked? Susmit runs to a house nearby and frantically knocks. He must get indoors before the demonic wind strikes again.The door opens and three young girls start laughing hysterically at Susmit. Susmit hears the rumbling of the wind again and runs to the next door and pushes at the bell with all his might. He pushes it again and again. Now he can film the wind is striking again and his last remaining piece of garment is being peeled off mercilessly. He can hear shouts of people who are clapping and shouting "Strip strip strip!"

And thanks to heaven at that point he wakes up from his drugged sleep. What a dream! He finds that he is perspiring and the bell of his apartment is ringing.

He answers the bell and opens the door to find Kasturi standing at the door. Susmit has not met Kasturi after that fateful party night. Why is she here? Has Mukherjee sent her to torment him in some new way? Susmit stands stupefied and even forgets to usher her in. Kasturi enters though and sort of collapses in a coach. She is looking very tired and drawn.

- Can I have glass of water Susmit?

Susmit pours her a glass of water and settles in the couch opposite to her.

- I give up Susmit. I have failed to forgive him. I had had a long inner battle. I have spent three consecutive sleepless nights. I cannot share my life with a man like this.
- But why are you taking such a decision for me? He has done wrong to me, not you.
- It's not that. That's not the whole truth. I have taken the decision for you, for Gopa, but above all for myself. If someone can stoop so low for the sake of professional jealousy he can do anything Susmit, just anything.
- You look tired. Would you like some coffee?
- You will make it?
- You can try...I believe I make good coffee.

Susmit returns with two mugs of coffee and some cookies. He is debating whether to ask or refrain from asking a question but decide to go for it.

- Have you thought of the danger Mukherjee may put you? He must be having intimate photos of you.
- I will not consider it danger, but it will be botheration though. Yes I have thought of it. In fact I know he will try to do it and will do it. It was a point of worry too.
- It was?
- Yes, it was, and not any more. I have crossed that hurdle. But just to prevent my nude photos being publicized I cannot let my life get ruined. After all me as person is far more important than my nude pictures.

Susmit heaves a sigh and lights a cigarette.

- Unfortunately Gopa could not take things in such logical manner.
- What!
- I have tried and tried and tried but failed. She is not marrying me.
- But why?! What was your fault?

Susmit sips his coffee and says, "Fault? Yes indeed I had one fault. I have made one grave mistake again and again".

- Mistake?
- I have urged her to be bold. She has posed to be bold but actually her traditional values etc. etc. were

always eating at her. She has only posed to be bold. I have not tried to understand her.
- If you permit I can talk to her. Remember we were buddies in college.
- No use. The ailment is deep down. Just like a few thousand feet under the ocean surface where there is perennial darkness.

A silence falls in the room. Two persons, a man and a woman are standing by the wrecks of their dreams woven over time and with much effort. They are there somewhat like the captains of the ships who look at the debris of shipwreck washed ashore and wonder why they have been so miraculously saved?

After some time, Susmit breaks the silence.

- But how can I keep on working with such a colleague? I think I should look for a job.

Kasturi smiles, "You can spare that effort. Your problem, rather our problem, will get solved soon."

- But how?
- You know our company's policy of zero tolerance towards sexual harassment to women. Mukherjee has sent lewd photos of women with juicy remarks to a number of our female colleagues? They will definitely complain.
- But why has he done such a thing?
- He has not done anything. I did. I had his laptop and his mail account could be casily accessed. Then

I have returned his laptop and told him that we are not getting married. The job was easy as he had a good collection of porn in his machine.

- But why ...why have you done it?

Susmit is feeling tense and relieved at the same time.

- He has made your life hellish. He will try to do so with mine. So a little act of retaliation was necessary, isn't it so?

Susmit takes a little time to answer. Actually he needed that time.

So ultimately the demon is killed! Then he utters almost inaudibly, "Great!!"

Kasturi gets up. She has to return now.

- Susmit tomorrow after your office I will take you to a new joint, it is called Mud Hut. They serve real good Brazilian coffee. The coffee you served, I am sorry to say, was terribly bad!

Susmit gives a hearty laugh, after a long time.

He says, "Please wait a minute. I will fetch the keys. I should drop you home."

A Night in Past Tense

I am Abhijit Sen, twenty nine, and working as deputy general manager of a multinational organization. I believe that I have reached such a position so early in my career because I was a good student and I am a workaholic. People think I toil so much and have made my job a part of my being because I love my job. It's totally nonsense. I have to keep myself busy as there is a huge chasm in my life which I need to keep covered up. I practically have no friends as I have observed so called friendly discussions very soon turn to rather thinly veiled contests of material achievements.

Besides my work there is something else I love, that is playing my violin. Needless to say that I play alone.I and my wife live in separate rooms. I start playing at late nights with the door of my room closed. The stagnant air of the closed room seems to get cut into pieces by the high pitched sound of my violin. I similarly feel a cutting pain deep down which can neither be explained nor do I need to.

My company owns a few mines in a place called Deoghar. I have to visit the mines from time to time and this time also I had gone on one such visit. While coming to Deoghar my chauffer Baramdao suddenly fell ill at Seuri which is somewhat midway from Kolkata to Deoghar. Fortunately he has got a relative in Seuri town and so I decided to drop him at the care of the relative and drive the rest of the road myself. Baramdeo wanted to arrange a local chauffeur but I decided to drive myself.

Next day when I finished my business at the mines it was past five. The manager of mines requested me to spend another night in local guest house and start in the morning. I was almost conceding to the idea when suddenly I remembered something that made me change my mind. Before I took to the wheels I have read the newspaper and have not even left out the daily almanac. Today is a full moon day. The roadahead has got no streetlight so this is a prized opportunity to enjoy a moonlit night. Driving alone in a moonlit night in a hilly road where traffic is scarcecan be an experience of a lifetime and I was the last person to let it go so easily. I have of course heard that there are some thieves and robbers who operate in this region but that's not enough to deter me from taking the tour at night. I am a bit more daring than the common folk and also I am not exactly unarmed. I have a four inch barrel Colt magnum anaconda which is as deadly as its namesake. The manager offered to give me dinner in a parcel which also I declined. As per my calculations I will take about three hours to reach the town of Burdwan where I will spend the night in some hotel.

When I start there was some light but soon darkness drops. Here darkness literally drops and very suddenly. It seemed as if a black veil is dropped on the hills and the road. But though I say darkness because of the moonlight everything around was looking very serene and almost dreamy. After some time I am almost forced to turn off the car stereo. It seemed too out of place for the surroundings I am passing through. Actually no sound other than the natural ones can be tolerated here. There is of course the low monotonous groan of the car engine but somehow it is not disturbing me. The road meanders through the hills. On my left is the hill, rising from the edge of the road and on my right are fields that seem to stretch till the horizons. At times I can see some dots of light passing by on my right and quite at a distance from the road. They are actually villages. I slow down to light a cigarette when suddenly an abrupt sharp noise makes me temporarily unnerved.

Then I realize it is nothing but a night owl. Probably old man owl is not happy to see the light of my car as it has disturbed his predatory ventures. After all it is working time for him. My radium watch says it is only seven PM. Actually there is no measure of night in these places. It is either day or night.

Not that the road is completely devoid of people. At times I can see a man or a man and a womanwalking along the edge with loads of twigs collected from the woods. In fact just like the sound of the stereo of my car, to them I am equally out of place.

This hill must have existed hundreds of years ago and there must have been such people living around doing the very same things as being done today by their predecessors. Here time has stopped. So called progress of civilization has got little meaning here. If someone comes here like me in a car after two hundred years, it's most likely that he would find the very same sort of people doing the same things. (Only of course the car would change.) When my car is passing they are looking at my car but not with much of interest. The detachment of these people from so called modern lives is very much apparent from their nonchalant attitudes. They are either walking and humming some local tune or contentedly chatting with their beaus. I have turned off my mobile phone. I am not in a mood to be disturbed. And also I have turned off the headlights of my car. Who needs any light when the whole world is flooded by such bright moonlight?

I am definite that such environment is perfect settings for romance at least in romantic novels. But this sort of seems very funny to me. When it comes to man woman romance I do not think any particular setting is necessary. Long back when I was in college I had had crush for a lady called Arunima. On a monsoon day we were returning from college in a public bus when the bus suddenly stopped and it was announced that we would have to vacate the bus as it had broken down. Kolkata in monsoon is hellish as water logging is very common. We did get down amidst torrential rain and suddenly Arunima's umbrella also called it a day like the bus. I naturally took the opportunity of offering her my umbrella. Then we waded through the water which was almost knee height sharing one umbrella, both getting drenched but laughing and cracking jokes, enjoying our miseries. In fact we both felt hungry and bought some food from a way side vendor who was selling his stuff standing in the same water. Though nothing did materialize and I donot know even where she is now, I believe it was the most romantic evening of my life.

I suddenly put the brakes and the car jerks to a stop. My briefcase kept in the back seat falls to the floor. I was, too engrossed in my thought so I didn't notice the man and the woman standing in the middle of the road. An aboriginal boy is standing with his girlfriend locked in embrace. I quickly embark and seek apology to them. Really driving with headlights off was height of folly. But the young man doesn't seem to be cross and seeks apology to be on the road like that. The girl is also embarrassed but smiles sweetly. I offer a cigarette to the man and ask him where they live. Because of my mines and frequent visits I can speak grammatically incorrect local language. They say that they live in a nearby village and have been married only a few months. They like strolling in the moonlight and so they were there. The man thanked me again and again for the cigarette and apologized once again and I start my journey again.

I have still about two hours of drive before I reach Burdwan. The young man is so happy just to get a cigarette...I can't help an out of place comparison with the reactions I get from my wife Gargi when I bring her so many expensive gifts. I have never found her really happy. Yes we stay in the same apartment as husband and wife should. We don't fight and she is otherwise a perfect homemaker. But somehow I feel there is a huge gap somewhere, I cannot exactly relate to her nor can she to me. I have noticed that she is perfectly normal with all matters except matters relating to marriage and man woman relationship. At times I feel she is living her life an enclosure created by walls, the walls made of ice, just as hard and just as cold. I have tried a lot but have failed to bring down that wall.

Now several trucks are coming from the opposite end and the drivers I must say are driving pretty recklessly. At times I am hearing a low bark; this is from an animal of cat family which are found in these localities. I heard such a call from quite close but before it totally died down a soundstarted that made a cold wave run down my spine. The noise is coming from my car engine and no other sound in the world can be more unwelcome in this situation.

I have run out of gas!

Baramdeo must have thought of refilling in Siuri but that was not possible. I should have checked the meter before starting which I didn't. Anyway, I park the car at the side of the road and embark. I am now near the river dam at Massanjore. I spot a shanty beside the dam gate, lock my car and walk towards it. It is actually a restaurant for the workers. At this hour there is no customer and the young chap is planning to close it for the day. The boy assures that if I pay in advance he can prepare me some food. Also he can manage some gas for my car in the morning of course and at a premium price.

Both propositions sound well but right now what I need is somewhere to put up for the night. As far as I know that though this is sort of a picnic spot there is no hotel to check in. The boy of the shop said that there are two guest houses but they won't allow stay without prior bookings. But there is a Youth Hostel where his uncle works as care taker and he will open a room if I 'make him happy'. Well I don't seem to have much of a choice so ask him the direction of the youth Hostel. The boy offers to deliver my dinner to the Youth

Hostel. I open the boot of my car collect the small suitcase lock my car and start walking towards my rendezvous for the night.

I find the Youth Hostel presently and rather suddenly. Just after taking a turn a little distance away from the shop the Youth Hostel situated on top of a hillock sort of springs up before my eyes. The Youth hostel resembles a small castle like the ones we see in the history books and is also made of stones. There is no light anywhere. The moon being behind the building the doorway is totally dark. I realize that I have left my cell phone behind in the car and as a heavy wind is blowing lighting my lighter would be of no use. I somewhat grope my way and call out for thecaretaker. The situation is very much like that described in De la Mare's poem, "Is there anybody there?" I called thrice but none of the doors or windows opened.

What is the matter? Has the caretaker gone to some village and making merry in some tavern? It seems quite likely, who in the world would like to stay here and take care where there is not much to take care of.

"You need a place to sleep, isn't it so Sahib?"

I almost jump up hearing the voice behind me. I have not noticed when or how this man covered almost entirely in a dark shawl has managed to come and stand behind me. Before I can say anything the man says again, "I can spare a room for you but you will have to leave early. Tomorrow a government official of the tourist department will come for inspection".

I have no plans to wait till late so it suits me fine. I hand him a hundred rupee note and he opens a dormitory for me and prepares a bed. He also provides some drinking water in a plastic jug and a fat candle and shows me the way to the toilet and I feel really indebted to him.

The room has fifteen beds and one cupboard dedicated for each occupant situated at the end of each bed. The walls, as much as visible in candle light, are home for hundreds of spiders. From the dust gathered everywhere it seems that there has been no visitor in few years. There are two windows at the two ends of the room. I open them. No doubt it will be cold with the windows open but still it is better than being gagged by the dust. From one of the windows I can see the dam and the lights shining there. As the lock gates are now closed there is no movement of water. The series of lamps mirrored in still water is creating a serene but sort of sad spectacle. A cool breeze blowing into the room is making me shiver a little. The flame of the candle is flickering in the breeze. With the breeze comes the noise of dried leaves being blown away. So far I was enjoying the loneliness but suddenly I start feeling restless. It is okay to be lonely by choice but being lonely by compulsion is no joke.

The unwavering lights mirrored in still water of the dam remind me of the sad look in Gargi's eyes. I am ready to pay a fortune if only I can take that look away from her eyes and see her smiling radiantly. I have taken her to psychiatrists and counselling centres but nothing has helped. I feel sad and move to the other window. On this side is the road meandering up to the 'castle'. But what's that? I see lights and then I realize some people approaching the Youth Hostel with blazing torches. Who can they possibly be? What do they want here? Now I can spot some of them are carrying long spears.

Robbers! I don't have much cash with me but still I have the car and the Rado watch I am wearing is quite costly. They must have been tipped off by the caretaker. I take out my Colt anaconda and then I realize my mistake.

It is the boy of the shanty restaurant and he has brought my dinner. He says it is not advisable to move alone at night so he has brought his friends. I finish my dinner and sit in a broken chair near the window and light a cigarette. The caretaker bids good night and promises to wake me up in the morning.

Drim Drim Dridim Dridim...I can hear the distant drum, must be coming from the some village in the hills. The music is crude but has got lot of warmth in it. It is not like the electronic lifeless but perfect music we hear all the time. When I was in college I did attend a survey session with my cronies guided by two of our professors. We had gone to a hilly village where the inhabitants were of Santal tribe. We used to spend our days measuring and recording data with theodolite and tapes. And in some of the evenings the tribal men and women used to gatherfor their community dance. The women, dark as mahogany, were of superb built and so were the men.

The rhythm of their dance had a tantalizing effect which was increased many fold by 'Mahua' or the liquor created from a fruit found locally. Though in these community dances groups performed together a little observation did easily revealed the 'couples'.

I have everything in life but completely deprived of a woman's love. At times, honestly speaking, I have indulged in the thought of divorce and starting afresh. Two pieces of furniture can spend ages kept side by side but not two human beings. But then I realized that it would be wrong, gravely so, to divorce her. She is also suffering in her own way and I as the husband need to give her more time. But the problem is logic doesn't seem logical all the time. Like right now the noise of the drum is making me very restless. I can see the men and women laughing and dancing together.

I get up from bed. I have insomnia and also I am not used to sleeping in this room. My car is lying unattended in the open road. It is adding to my worries and making the possibility of having some sleep even more remote. And to top it all there is the incessant beating of the drum. I am longing for some reading material. I have left a paperback novel in the glove box of my car. It is not practical to venture to go out and bring it now. From some noise I understand that I am not alone in the room in strict sense. There are rats that must be living here undisturbed for years.

The place being so lonely it deepens the desire for human company. In fact I wish the caretaker was here so that I could talk, just to listen to some human voice.

It is absolutely unethical to read someone's personal diary but I did so once. I did read a few pages of Gargi's diary. The cheap television commercials at times have sequences when the wife or the husband is reading other's diary to find out his or her illicit affairs. For me it was different. I just wanted to know her, to break through the wall where she is serving a life sentence. Very honestly unlike the television serials I would have been happy to find that she has a lover and she islonging for him. At least it would have proved she belongs to a sphere of the world that I know. What I found instead is a page full of lamenting and apologizing to someone she mentioned as 'Shi'. Who this 'Shi' is or why was Gargi so apologetic there was no means to understand.

Now it one AM. After a few hours the dawn will break. But unfortunately for Gargi it is sort of eternal night, no light, no desire, just like those pathetic lines of 'Mariana in the South'

"The night comes on that knows not morn,
When I shall cease to be all alone,
To live forgotten, and love forlorn."

I am walking up and down the room. I believe by now I have walked for at least a few kilometres. Suddenly I discover a fat book lying at the corner of the room. I take it up, dust it as far as possible and bring it near the candle. I find it is a visitors' book where the guests have left their impressions. The last entry is about five years old. Some of the entries are quite interesting, like some Vicky has written. "Got rugs with bed bugs". Some have even tried their hands in sketching. It's obvious that most of the people or groups came from colleges.

What a life I also had in my college days! College excursions, bunking classes and going for movies, the charged up college union elections and so many interesting things I had to fill my days. I am getting quite nostalgic.

Suddenly a folded piece of paper drops to the floor from the folds of the visitors' book. I casually pick it up, unfold it and a shiver runs my spine.

I know this hand writing!

The paper has yellowed with age; the pen with which the writing was done was a poor one still the familiarity is just unmistakable. The date at the top right corner is a day about six years back. How strange! So Gargi had come here and spent timein this room. I make a quick calculation, then she was twenty, that means she also might have come in college group.

The candle is now almost dying down still I start reading.

"I can never forgive myself for what happened today. I am responsible. I am responsible. I didn't want to come to this excursion...why did I come. He told me not to get into the waters, but still I wished to show off and got in...Then suddenly I felt that I am getting lost...being drawn into the waters more and more...the current was so strong...he jumped into the water but could not manage to save himself. I feel like dying...I feel like going to the river and jump. It will take moments for me to die. But how can I die now? Shibasish has saved me and has made my life even more valuable.." The candle flickers twice and goes off. I bring out the lighter from my pocket with my hand trembling, light it and continue reading.

"..His body has been found a few miles downstream. I could not look at the face, but when I did it seemed that he was smiling that familiar smile and at any moment he will call out - silly girl don't worry I am here! Tomorrow her parents are arriving. What will I tell them? How can I ever face the world again? Forgive me Shi, please forgive me...how could you leave your silly girl like this..."

So Gargi had come here from her college and was about to get drowned in the river when Shibashis saved him. That's why she is living a life of eternal mourning, constantly blaming herself for the death of Shi. I suddenly feel restless; I need to go to Kolkata, now. I need to be with her, reason with her, help her.

I come out of the room. The dawn is breaking slowly but still it is dark and misty. I look at the hills and find chain of fires burning. The tribal people have gathered the dry leaves and put fire to the piles. The fire has formed a thin chain that is running from one hill to another hill.

Gargi is burning in a similar fire.

No parched skin, no smoke, no smell, yet the fire rages on and on.

The Depths of the Atlantic

Ayan Chatterjee seated in economy class of flight A380-800 to Dubai turned off his cell phone, put it in the side pocket of his jacket and prepared to go for a long slumber. Long flights are somehow extremely boring and sleeping is perhaps the only respite.

The airlines do offer various distracters like movies and music but somehow Ayan has found he can never be comfortable watching movies in air. The flight time to Dubai is seven hours and then there is a layoff of about four hours. Then he will catch the flight to Kolkata. Ayan's seat is second from the window. The window seat is still vacant. The man seated to the left of Ayan is an aged Indian, likely Gujarati, grumpy in look and has already engrossed himself in a business magazine. Somewhere Ayan had read that people having seats in the middle in movie theatres always arrive last. It now seemed that the saying is correct because the lady approaching his row must be the claimant of the window seat by his side. Ayan has already looked back and found no other seat is vacant in the rows behind him.

"Excuse me" the lady has arrived.

Ayan and the Gujarati gentleman get up to make way for her. These days the leg space kept by the airlines companies makes it sort of imperative. The lady in blue tea shirt and faded jeans thanks Ayan and the other gentleman and settles herself. Almost at the same time the crew closed the door of the aircraft.

The lady is in mid-thirties, almost at the same age of Ayan, a bit heavy set and wears glasses. She takes out an English novel from a small bag, tucks it to the side of her seat and prepares to read. Ayan turns his attention to other passengers. Observing the reactions of passengers particularly just before take-off can be very interesting. Some people who have Aviophobia try to keep themselves busy. Like for example the middle aged gentleman in the left row is trying hard toread a fashion magazine but even the photos of scantily clad beautiful women are not being able to hold his attention as every now and then he is either looking at his watch or looking out of the window. A Muslim gentleman a few rows ahead is saying his prayers and so is an aged lady who must be an Indian.

"Oops!" the lady beside her has dropped her book. Ayan picks it up for her. He notes the book is 'Hungry tides' by Amitava Ghosh.

"Thanks" smiles the lady, "I am Paula Anderson."
"Ayan Chatterjee" replies Ayan "I am from the same city as the author of this novel"
"Oh Kolkata! Very exotic place"

Ayan feels good to hear something good about his native city.

"You are going to Kolkata?" asks Paula.

"Yes, going back after about ten years".

"I was born in India you know, Delhi actually. My father used to work in the high commission. I have been to Kolkata once, when I was about, well, seventeen or eighteen."

Paula disclosed that she was in India till she was nineteen and then her father moved back to UK. She is now working for an NGO that operates internationally and her work is taking her to Kolkata.

Ayan takes out the print out of the email from his pocket and reads it for the fifty third time. This is his first visit to Kolkata after settling in UK about ten years back. The email is short and crisp.

> "Sanghamitra expired after suffering a car crash last Sunday. We will be holding a memorial service for her on the fifth of October at 17:30 hrs in Tyagraj Hall. Will be glad if you can manage to come.
>
> Regards,
> Bikash"

Bikash is the husband of Sanghamitra, and Sanghamitra is the reason why Ayan is living a life in exile. These ten years he has neither heard nor tried to contact Sanghamitra or her husband, and now by strange turn of events he is flying few thousand miles to attend her 'memorial service'.

The term 'memorial service' seems quite funny to Ayan. Some people gathering to think of and speak of someone who had had an untimely death and people call it a 'service'! Whom are they serving, and the person for whom all will be gathering is beyond any terrestrial or extra-terrestrial service limit? The term is so dispassionate; it reeks of sense of duty with lot of botheration attached.

Ayan did call up Bikash receiving the email. Actually Bikash didn't have Ayan's mail ID, so he did send the mail to administration of the Kolkata office of Ayan's company and they have redirected the message to him. The fatal car crash did occur on a flyover. Sanghamitra was driving the car and she was alone. Sanghamitra survived for twenty four hours after the crash. Twice did she regain consciousness and both times she did ask for Ayan. She could not recognize her husband or son Indrajit. Ayan could sense very well that Bikash was not exactly comfortable in inviting him to the function. For a day or two Ayan toyed with the decision of whether or not he should be attending the function. After all there is a risk of becoming centre of curiosity for some gossip mongers, but then he consented.

Ideally speaking the fact that Sanghamitra Saha is no more should not matter to him. For him Sanghamitra has died long back.

Here Ayan's chain of thoughts stumbles and pauses for some time. Is it so? Has Sanghamitra died long back for Ayan? Or is it just the other way round. Sanghamitra was alive and so much so that Ayan could never think of coming to Kolkata all these years. A city is defined geographically for all official purposes but actually each one has got his or her own definition of a city, and this definition is emotionally geographical.

For Ayan Kolkata meant Southern avenue, Lake Market, Film Festival, Dover Lane Music Conference, Academy of Fine Arts and the strand beside the Ganges. And with all these places there are number of memories of Sanghamitra.

"Sir, tea or Coffee?" the airhostesses have started their rounds.

"Coffee" answers Ayan.
"What do you like more, tea or coffee?" Sanghamitra had asked. Ayan always prefers coffee.

"Why do you prefer coffee? Give me five reasons." She was never happy with a short answer.

Ayan gave it a thought and then started
"To begin with Coffee has a kick which tea doesn't have, secondly the aroma of coffee is much more appealing, thirdly, coffee creates an excitement, fourthly, coffee is much more macho and and..." Ayan groped for the fifth reason.
"And?" Sanghamitra was all ears.

"And, because you make excellent coffee" Ayan landed up being personal as he had no other answer. The conversation was taking place in a car with Sanghamitra at the wheels. Normally Sanghamitra did the driving when they were together. According to Sanghamitra Ayan's driving was too rash and could not be relied upon. They were going to

Digha in a weekend. They had slowed down as a herd of cows were blocking the way and the shepherd was taking time in clearing the road.

"This was actually a psychological test. I studied you and I have understood." said Sanghamitra.

"What have you understood dear psychologist?"

"I have understood that you are sexually very aggressive!"

Ayan did give a hearty laugh. He was on the verge of saying why did Sanghamitra need a psychology test to understand his attitude towards sex but refrained. Sanghamitra was like that, apparently very serious but actually extremely childish.

"You have your family in Kolkata?" suddenly asks Paula.

"No, as such I have no family".

"Must be having a girlfriend whom you are going to marry soon?" Paula gives an impish smile.

"Unfortunately no; I am a loner"

"Strange!" Paula is very much astonished, "But why? You are not crazy?"

"Probably I am" smiles Ayan "What about you?"

"I have married twice but right now I am single" replies Paula Anderson.

"Then why are you so astonished to see that I am single and without any girlfriend" asks Ayan.

"Because" answers Paula, "You Indians love to get married and stay married."

Snacks have been served and Paula gets busy in eating. Ayan is in no mood to eat now. He thinks of the last words of Paula, "get married and stay married." How correct she is.

He also did yearn to get married and certainly he would have stayed married...but...

When he first migrated to UK he had had a terrible time. The nights were particularly very tormenting. He had not communicated his UK phone number to Sanghamitra. Many a time he had thought of picking up the phone and calling her but he never did. Instead he sat near the phone, stone drunk, waiting and waiting for it to ring. He knew that his actions were pure folly, miracles do not occur in real world but still could not help sitting near the phone for hours. At times he would pick up the receiver and dial the number of his Kolkata home 0091-33-4803947 and had disconnected as soon as the phone at the other end began to ring.

Then slowly his new life had entered him. He had made himself extremely busy with his work, with the parties, booze and girls. He had had no romantic feeling towards any of the girls though. Just as scenes fade out in a movie, all the scenes like Lake Market, Kolkata Film Festival, Dover Lane, 4803947 had faded away.

"Hey Sir! Are you alright?" Paula is lightly shaking his shoulder.

Ayan feels a bit embarrassed. "Yeah, why?"
"Actually you were talking in your sleep. I heard some numbers 480...3...9 something. Oh...you have tears in your eyes!"

Ayan understands that he must pull himself together. He goes to washroom, splashes cold water to his face and comes back to his seat. He is feeling better now.

"You loved this Sanghamitra...isn't it so?" Paula suddenly asks. Then she confesses that Ayan's print out had fallen off from his pocket and she has read it. She apologized for reading it.

Suddenly Ayan feels that he needs to talk. All these years he has never ever talked of Sanghamitra and his relation with her. And to say all these there can be nobody better than Paula. They have met only in the aircraft and after a few hours they will part and in all likelihood will never see each other again. Ayan makes up his mind.

"Excuse me Paula, if you don't mind can you give me some time? I need to say something."
Paula consented in the most compassionate manner possible.

*   *   *

When Ayan first met Sanghamitra, she was already married. Her husband Bikash joined the company as deputy manager and was in the same department as Ayan. At that time Ayan was tremendously interested in drama and was organizing a play for the office annual function. He did the lead in the play. A few days after the annual function Ayan received a call from Sanghamitra. After formal introduction Sanghamitra invited him to dinner at her home in the weekend ahead. She said that Ayan can't refuse on any pretext as this dinner was 'a tribute to Ayan's direction and own performance in the play'.

Ayan did keep the invitation. Little did he know that he was embarking on a new chapter that would change the entire story of his life?Actually the fact that keeps human life interesting is the total unpredictability that a new dawn will bring with it. Ayan could feel that very first day that his hosts, Bikash and Sanghamitra actually do not sync with each other. Bikash turned out to be a diehard drunkard and a man of very coarse taste. Any man with reasonable amount of sensitivity would prefer being alone for days to his company. His jokes were as filthy as his smelly mouth. Sitting face to face but a few feet apart was also painful.

On the other hand, Sanghamitra was suave, erudite and had a mark of class in anything she did. She proved to be a fantastic cook as well. That day Sanghamitra was dressed in a pale yellow sari and Ayan felt that the colour of her Sari was somewhat symbolic. Actually she was like fresh green grass turning pale as grass turns pale if put under a brick.

After that they did meet several times in office parties or in some marriage ceremony of some colleague. Each meeting was different as with each meeting they felt more and more drawn to each other and then they started meeting clandestinely.

They used to go to plays at Academy of Fine Arts, went to concerts, never missed some newly released movie that elicited their interest and of course their favourite restaurants.

Peter Cat in Park Street was the most favourite joint and that was bound to be the place on special occasions.

"Sir, what would you like to have?" the pretty lady has come with her cart of drinks.
"Lime cordial" Ayan practically blurts out.

The air hostess serves the drink and turns her attention to the bulky man sitting beside Ayan. Paula cannot hide her astonishment at Ayan's choice. Ayan blushes. He says that as that was the fixed order for Sanghamitra in Peter Cat, and he was talking of their visits to Peter Cat Ayan has said that almost automatically.

Paula smiles and takes a sip from her glass of whisky on the rocks.

At times Ayan was really surprised at the attitude of Sanghamitra, she seemed to throw caution to the winds at times. After all she was a married woman. Ayan was tremendously surprised when Sanghamitra came up with the proposal of making a trip to Digha, a sea resort some one hundred and twenty five miles away from Kolkata.

Sanghamitra said that she wanted to make the trip in Ayan's car. On the way Ayan asked how Sanghamitra had planned to tackle the problem of Bikash. Chances were high that he would strongly suspect something.

Its common human nature when someone puts a question he anticipates one or more probable answers. In general cases the answer matches or nearly matches one of the alternatives.

In this case the answer when it came was so unexpected that cigarette he was smoking dropped off Ayan's lips.

Sanghamitra said, "No question of 'if'. I have left a note on the bedside cabinet informing where I am going and also the phone number of the hotel in case of any emergency. Why should I hide anything? He is in no position to stop me from what I want to do."

"You sound so platonic in your tale" Paula is a bit high after three pegs, "you mean to say that it was all like that all along?"

A bath in the sea needs to be followed by a shower in clean water. The whole morning, in fact starting from early morning, they were in the sea beach. Twice or thrice they had gone into water and had floated for long times with the waves. Sanghamitra was ecstatic just like a teenager. She was laughing and throwing water at Ayan. Ayan warned her repeatedly not to move far from the shore. She was teasing Ayan saying that she wanted to go much into the sea. Many a time Ayan had embraced his lady love but embracing the same person in water with shifting sand below the feet was a totally different experience. It sortof symbolized life with the water standing for the turmoil we are always in and the shifting sand saying that nothing is permanent.

Then they returned to their hotel. Ayan settled in the couch with a coffee and Sanghamitra went for shower. A little later he could hear her voice as she was singing in the shower. Ayan tried hard to calm his mind and to think of ethics but gave up after some time. The temptation was too much.

He had noticed that from the balcony a window to the bathroom was quite close and could be peeped into. He tried that but was not successful. The window was closed. Through the frosted glass he could make out the form of her lady but that was not enough. He came back and went near the door of the bathroom and had a pleasant surprise.

Sanghamitra has forgotten to bolt the door!
Slowly Ayan pushed through the door. Sanghamitra was startled and got stupefied. She had even forgotten to pull the long towel kept quite close and cover her nudity. The shower was still running. Ayan felt that he was looking at Venus standing under a stream. Droplets of water were flowing down the beautiful female form. She was exceptionally fair and artistically curvy.

After this Ayan went into a trance or that's what he feels when he thinks of that moment. The details cannot be recollected. When he came back to somewhat near reality both of them were lying in the floor, the shower still running, two bodies till locked with each other. They actually never discussed their future course of action. It was quite clear to both though that they could not continue to live without each other.

The call made from Kolkata at around ten at night the same day was like a bolt from the blue. Bikash had been admitted to a hospital in critical condition. He was suffering from acute stomach ache and was vomiting blood. Sanghamitra drove like a crazy person and they covered the distance in almost half the usual time. The doctor said that he had cirrhosis of lever and was in acritical stage. But the real crisis struck not then but after two days.

Sanghamitra said that she could not leave Bikash as he was so pathetically ill. She felt that even if Bikash managed to pull through the acute crisis he would have to live a very restricted life and would constantly require the care of Sanghamitra. She said that had it been otherwise she would have made a clean breast of facts to Bikash and leave him. But given the circumstances the same was not possible.

"How silly! Was she crazy?" asks Paula
Ayan had had the same query in her mind when he first heard all these from Sanghamitra. But he showed infinite patience and reasoned with her again and again. And he did win.

Gradually as Bikash recovered Sanghamitra was also able to see logic in Ayan's words. Truly speaking two recovery processes were running simultaneously. She did agree to leave Bikash and marry Ayan. But she did put forward a condition. Ayan would have to arrange to take her away to some far away land. She believed that Bikash's illness was sure to relapse and he would die a very sorry death. She wanted to be far away from the scene. Fortunately for Ayan a few days before all these his company did offer Ayan to take charge of their new office in London.

Everything was arranged within a few days. Sanghamitra did come to Ayan's house and helped him with the packing. Ayan had lost his parents long back and had planned to leave the house in the care of an old servant who had been serving in his house since Ayan was a kid.

Their flight from Kolkata was at eight in the evening. In the night before the day of departure Sanghamitra again changed her mind. By this time Bikash had recovered to a great deal but yet she felt it would be a 'crime' to leave him like that.

This time Ayan could not show any further patience because he had none left. He only said that Sanghamitra should let him know by five PMthe following day if she changed her mind. Ayan sat beside his land phone from ten in the morning to five PM and then when he had to leave.

There was no call from Sanghamitra.
He locked the room and left for the airport. Actually with leaving the room and locking it he had sort of left the life he had dreamt.

"So that was my story" laughs Ayan, "you see after all I could not win her." Paula only smiled and said nothing.

When the announcement of landing was being made she shared her London address as well as her cell number with Ayan. She will be spending two days in Dubai where she has some business and so won't be able to accompany Ayan on his flight from Dubai to Kolkata. After that of course she will be coming to Kolkata and from there fly back to UK through the same route.

Before alighting from the aircraft she only said, "It is not correct to lose faith on anything or one's own self. I have suffered losses twice but haven't lost faith."

* * *

Ayan comes back to his room and opens it after ten years. Though the house was taken care of, the room being locked has become dusty with cobwebs hanging here and there. He lovingly looked at his room, his abode of memories. His books, his guitar all are under a coat of dust. He comes and sits in his favourite chair. The chair creaked in protest for being jolted out of slumber like that of Rip Van Winkle. The telephone kept on the table is inoperative. The authorities have disconnected the line as they always do for defaulters.

But what's that?

A cold wave strong and crippling flows through Ayan's spine. The telephone receiver is not kept properly in the cradle! Even if the lines were working people calling this number would have found it 'engaged'!

Ayan remembers that on the day of his leaving his cell phone was switched off at around twelve as the battery had run out of charge. He didn't bother to charge it as he knew it was going to have no use after a few hours. What a fool he had been thinks Ayan.

Who knows whether Sanghamitra had changed her mind and had tried to call him? A few days after leaving for UK a colleague from Kolkata had reported that shortly after

Ayan had left Bikash had had another crisis. That crisis might have started the very day they were supposed to leave together...who knows?

But who will answer all these today? Sanghamitra is beyond the reach of all telecommunication systems of the world.

Did she look for Ayan after the accident as she wanted to tell why she could not come?

The caretaker hears a noise and runs to the room.

To his utmost surprise he finds Ayan lying in the dust and crying pathetically.

* * *

Ayan is going back today. He is seated in the aircraft beside Paula. Actually after spending two days in Kolkata Ayan felt that he had to leave and otherwise he would go crazy. He contacted Paula and planned to go back together. No, he won't stay back for the memorial service. The burden of memories he has is already crushing him, he can take no more. In the flight from Dubai when the plane was crossing the Atlantic Ayan felt this time he is really leaving his country. So long part of him, was in Kolkata.

Down below looking at the waters he felt for centuries so many ships and vessels have got lost forever in the ocean. Nobody will ever see them. His affair with Sanghamitra and many known and unknown facts will similarly remain buried forever.

The Evil

The letter has been received by Chhabi, Ruchira's combined hand. Ruchira found the letter waiting for her when she settled down for her second tea-session after Rana left for office. A letter from one Mr. Chhetri, the solicitor engaged by Kamalika to take care of Kamalika's will.

A letter or a bomb in disguise!

Ruchira knew her friend Kamalika's days were numbered – she had been suffering from Leukaemia, but she didn't know that the end was so near.Anyway, it's better to board the train than sitting in the waiting room with bated breath-- that's how Ruchira tried to console herself. This demise is sad but bearable but it is the other news conveyed in the letter that is making a cold wave run down her spinal cord.

Ruku is coming and he will be staying with Ruchira and Rana!

Ruku was only one month old when Ruchira last saw him. In-fact Ruchira has never tried to know anything about Ruku after that. Kamalika must have had noticed Ruchira's aversion in discussing Ruku, and true to herself Ruchira is ashamed of her behaviour, but she was undone. The very remembrance of Ruku has always made her shudder. If

Ruchira ever had psychology in her curriculum she would have recognized this as 'defence mechanism'.

This is strange, Ruchira admitted to herself, but again this is reality. Ruchira had tried to shut-off any memory of Ruku, as if simply forgetting him will render him unreal!

Ruchira remembered once she had read a novel 'Man woman and child' by Erich Segal, which dealt with somewhat similar situation. But the situation at hand is far more crucial since here Ruchira is the errant and the country is India!

This is the fourth year of Ruchira's marriage and she is yet to conceive. After various consultations with different physicians Rana has almost given up any hope, and these days he is talking of going for adoption. All these years Ruchira has dreaded doctors like anything. For her a visit to a doctor means added tension, frustration and above all extreme humiliation. Always she has to take the doctor into her confidence, and whisperingly tell him about her past and plead him not to divulge anything to her husband. Nothing can be more demeaning.

Rana is thinking of adopting a male child, Ruchira thought, so the idea of adopting the son of Ruchira's deceased friend may be not too difficult for him to accept. That is Ruchira's only hope for the time being. Ruchira finds herself profusely perspiring in this December morning. What if Rana does not accept Ruku? People normally adopt babies and not a child of six. Rana doesn't know Kamalika, Ruchira has never mentioned this friend of hers.

'I should have thought of this situation' Ruchira is blaming herself,' what a fool I had been! I knew of Kamalika's illness, I should have anticipated today's situation'.

Ding Dong…the calling bell.

It's Mrs. Senapati of 55B. She has come with her seven year old daughter to leave her keys with Ruchira. She is a typical house wife of an executive happy in her own stagnant life. She says she is going to her parental home and requests to give the keys to Mr. Senapati, as she will be returning late. Ruchira takes the keys and Mrs. Senapati leaves wondering what has befallen Ruchira? She seems to be dumbstruck.

Ruchira is actually shocked. Payel, Mrs. Senapati's daughter, looks exactly like her mother. How does Ruku look like? Wondered Ruchira. What if he looks exactly like his mother?

A night, seven years back has shattered the life of Ruchira. Everything happened so fast somewhat like a devastating tornado and has left a deep scar. That night often comes back in her nightmares. Only two days back she passed a ghoulish night. She felt like being crushed by an iron embrace, with hot breath burning her face. She felt its pitch dark and nothing is visible. Suddenly a solitary ray of light fell on her tormentor and she saw the face with piercing eyes, it opened its mouth and Ruchira saw to her horror its tongue is forked, it is a snake!

So many times Ruchira had thought she should tell Rana what had happened, but could never bring herself to do it. She so often feels guilty of not being able to bear a child.

The letter says Ruku will be arriving tomorrow, and Ruchira has to make a quick decision. Ruchira's sister Snigdha lives close by. Both she and her husband Bhaskar are teaching in the same college. Ruchira decides to consult Snigdha.

* * *

Ruchira and her classmates had lately been aware of a vicious group engaged in some sinister activities in the college. There had been some mysterious and sudden dropouts. Sunanda, the brightest boy of Chemistry Honours, suddenly started behaving in a strange manner. He stopped attending classes and started spending time with most rotten elements of the college. His disposition had suffered a severe change. Then one day, he fell ill in the college and he had to be rushed off to hospital. Ruchira and her friends went to the hospital to see Sunanda only to find him in a terrible dance of death.

Ruchira will never forget the scene in her life. Sunanda was going through severe convulsions, and screaming from excruciating pain – the pitiless lashings of cocaine. Sunanda died at the dead of night.

More than sense of grief or loss Ruchira and her friends felt deeply ashamed, after all Sunanda was their batch mate. The bright boy of Chemistry Honours, the blue eyed boy of the entire college left with lungs reeking with cocaine!

Before long the fact came to light that it was not Sunanda alone, quite a few students had had adopted similar deadly practices. A drug racket was running rife, and a few of the college students had joined hands with the drug peddlers.

The prime suspects were the group of Pintu, Sunny, Natu and others – the 'gems' of the college who used to adorn the same classes for years.

Ruchira and her friends drew a plan. Sabyasachi made acquaintance with the suspects and expressed interest in drugs. It was actually a trap well laid and the miscreants were caught red-handed. Principal Dr. Somdeb Dutta greatly helped to bring the miscreants to book. Though a police case was lodged against the errant boys, due to intervention of some 'prominent personalities' the cases were withdrawn and police had to release them. However their 'academic career' ended then and there.

The fatal incident occurred after a month or so. The Saraswati Puja arrived. As was the normal practice, Ruchira and her friends Sabyasachi, Pradyut, Arijit and Suchhanda planned to work throughout the night to complete the shrine along with all decorations. At around two they felt tired collectively and decided to go for a walk. The group consisted of three boys and two girls. They had planned to wake up a tea-vendor and get some tea. When they were close to the bridge on the narrow river 'Karola' Ruchira had an eerie sensation and did propos to go back. Her friends, however, laughed at her cowardice, and they continued the walk.

Suddenly four figures, with all their faces covered with black clothes, and carrying iron rods chains etc., leaped on them out of darkness. The boys were hit hard with the hardware and they lost consciousness. The ladies were carried to a dark shanty and were gang raped mercilessly. Suchhanda died the next day in the government hospital, and soon it was discovered that Ruchira had become pregnant! None of the miscreants could be identified and there were no arrests.

Ruchira could have gone for abortion, given her condition it would be legal too, but she denied to take any such step! Strangely she felt pity for her unborn child. Ruchira went to Kurseong to Kamalika, her senior crony from school days. Kamalika and her husband Nikhilesh were goodness personified. They took care of Ruchira and decided to adopt Ruchira's child. It was a safe delivery and Ruchira left for her home after a month of the childbirth, leaving her only child with Kamalika. Ruchira's father Bikashbabu had a transferable job and he got himself and his family transferred to Kolkata immediately after this incident.

Some time back Ruchira has read the news of murder of wildlife photographer Nikhilesh Sen by poachers. Kamalika has died of cancer, and Ruku is coming to stay with Ruchira!

* * *

Ruchira rings up Snigdha and explains her predicament. Snigdha is much more practical compared to Ruchira. She asks Ruchira to keep her cool and not to hastily disclose anything to her husband. 'No action can be taken before Ruku's arrival' opines Snigdha.

Ruchira comes to the balcony, the room is so stuffy. What will she do now? She is guilty, again she is not guilty. What else could she have done? What can a girl do in her situation? Will it be wise to tell everything to Rana?

No ..it's impossible. Rana is a strange character. Ruchira has never come across a more unpredictable man in her life. At times he is magnanimous and at times he is extremely narrow.

Suddenly Ruchira remembers something that sends a cold shiver down her spine. A girl named Paromita, daughter of an ill-tempered retired army officer lived in an adjacent flat with her parents. Paromita had had an affair and had got pregnant. When the retired army man came to know of her daughter's 'misdeed' he had chased her with open leather belt. The girl sought refuge in Ruchira's flat. But Rana simply turned her out right into the face of her father's mad fury. Ruchira was stunned. Later on Rana explained giving her refuge would be 'indulging' debauchery. Paromita was severely beaten up and had to be hospitalised.

How would such a man react to his own wife's 'immorally borne child'? Ruchira understands pretty well the fact she was wronged against would not hold much water with Rana.

Somehow Ruchira feels certain that Ruku would look exactly like Ruchira and Rana will understand the truth in no time. She things of the option of sending Ruku to some hostel or orphanage, (the thought however makes her ashamed) but that would require both time and money and Ruchira has none. Suddenly a terrible headache starts.

They are dancing round and round incessantly, gory looking Eunuchs, dressed in shocking colours chanting filthy rhymes in hoarse voices. These people always get the news of childbirth. Ruchira helplessly looks all around – suddenly the faces of the eunuchs change, all of them look exactly like Rana!

Ruchira gets up with a jerk. What a terrible dream! She remembers lying down for a while for the Aspirin to start action. How could she doze off in the midst of such anxiety?

* * *

Rana is a top notch executive of a construction farm. In recent days there were some problems with so called 'syndicates' who control the supply of building materials. Rana has used his exceptional manipulative powers to nail down the main man who was creating maximum trouble. The man is now in jail with charges of sexually assaulting his maidservant. This has earned Rana a promotion to the post of a full time Director of the Company. Rana has not stopped at that. He has exposed his colleague and arch rival Bose who was a felicitator of the syndicate business. Bose has been demoted.

Rana returns home. Today he is in exceptionally foul mood because Bose had come to Rana's chamber and called him an 'impotent man'! He starts rows with Ruchira over trifles and reaches the topic of Ruchira's childlessness in no time. He calls her 'barren – incapable of bearing any child ever'. Under normal circumstances Ruchira could never dream of disclosing her secret but today it is different, Ruchira shouts out that Rana is wrong and she has a child!

Ruchira has to disclose the incident. Rana patiently listens, without any visible agitation. When Ruchira finishes her account he passes the verdict. Ruchira will have to leave the very next morning. Rana's lawyers will take care of divorce proceedings. Needless to say Ruchira will have to take Ruku with her. Ruchira calmly accepts the verdict, and starts packing her suitcases. They have a silent dinner and go to sleep in different rooms.

Ruku arrives early morning the next day. Ruchira freezes when she sees Ruku.

Even a child can be sure of Ruku's parentage.
Ruku has striking resemblance with Rana!

Rana forgets to light his cigarette. He becomes extremely uneasy. Who in the world could have thought such would be the outcome of his misdeed?

Rana was promoting a project in Balurghat when his old cronies Natu and Pintu contacted him. They were to avenge the arrest and disclosure of the drug racketeers. Rana willingly agreed and actually enjoyed the 'revenge'. Rana had little option as he was earlier caught in bed by Natu with his cousin sister Krishna.

Ruchira's confession reminded him of his past misdeed but since Ruchira had spared the details he thought it to be a chance similarity.

Ruku starts taking food with his left hand – Rana is a lefty. Ruku has also inherited Rana's disturbing habit of squinting and flapping his eyelids frequently.

Ruchira looks straight in the eye of Rana and asks whether she can be granted one more day after which she will leave with the child. Rana avoids the gaze and says that Ruchira can stay as long as she wishes.

An unnerved Rana makes another blunder. He makes a call to Natu without noticing that Ruchira is within earshot!

* * *

Police detective Arunangshu Roy cannot think of any motive for murder and decides that it must have been suicide and sends Rana's body for autopsy.

Rana has been found dead in the bathtub with the electric hair dryer immersed in water. Rana has died of electrocution.

Ruchira had never used the hairdryer before but from now on, she decides she would use it. She thanks her luck that Rana had had the habit of going to the bathtub with the door open.

The story could well have ended here. But a small development occurs after this.

Ruchira is now in Kalimpong, teaching in the school where Kamalika used to teach. Ruku is very happy to get back in the midst of his friends.

Rana's relatives are fighting over his property and making the lawyers rich. Ruchira has forfeited all claims on the assets. She doesn't want the rapist's property for Ruku.

And lastly…these days Ruku calls Ruchira, 'Notun Ma' or new mom.

######################

The Valley of Shadow
of Death

To her extreme dismay Minu, a girl of seventeen has suddenly realized that she is sitting amidst a lot of people in a cheap tavern drinking and talking filthy and she is stark naked!

Minu doesn't know how she got there or why is she naked. She is terrified to find that though she should immediately get up and run for cover, she is unable to move her feet as if they are glued to the ground. Fortunately, if anything can be termed 'fortunate' in such a state, nobody seems to notice her. Minu lives in a nearby slum and is aware of this cheap tavern which is popularly known as Maqbool's Hotel as one Sheikh Maqbool owns it.

She is also not unfamiliar with men in stone drunk state as his own father Nirmal is a regular drunkard. But she cannot understand why and how she is going unnoticed sitting in such a state amidst all these men. Surely drinking reduces consciousness but definitely not to this level as a fully grown woman sitting stark naked can go unnoticed.

No, Minu realizes presently that she is not totally unnoticed.

In Maqbool's hotel drink is served on long tables running from one end of the room to the other. The customers sit in similarly long benches kept on both sides of the table. The tavern is quite full of people now as this must be the peak business hour. A bulky man in mechanic's uniform stained heavily with grease comes and asks Minu to move over as he wants a slot on the bench to sit. Minu moves over, terrified as she is, though there is hardly much place to move.

Suddenly Minu sees a piece of cloth lying on the table. She grabs it and tries to cover her breasts. Presently a waiter comes along and looks for the piece of cloth. Actually the piece of dirty cloth is meant for wiping the table. The waiter looks for the cloth here and there. He is sure that he has left it a few minutes back precisely at that point of the table and is surprised to see that it's not there. Suddenly he sees Minu holding the cloth with covering her breasts. He utters a filthy abuse and grabs the cloth. Minu holds at the cloth with all her might, after all it is all she has to cover her nakedness. But she is no match for the man, he snatches away the cloth utters another filthy abuse and walks away. Because of the tug of war Minu slips from the bench and falls to the ground.

Minu gets up. Oh what a bad dream it was! Still she is shivering from within. Once she had heard that dreams have meanings and can be analysed. She wonders if anyone she knows has the power of such analysis. Unfortunately her circle is too small and too blunt.

The room is dark. There is no light except some light from the lamp post coming through the torn curtain. Minu lives in a slum of Kumortuli area. She along with his father, sister and a brother sleeps in the same room. In fact this is the only room in their house, if it can be called a house. Father sleeps in a separate cot and all the brothers and sisters sleep in a bigger bed. Minu has lost her mother in her childhood and can hardly remember her.

She tries to get up, it is almost impossible to go back to sleep right away. She gropes in semi darkness towards the door and when she is near the door she hears a whine which is not natural in a room of sleeping people. Then she understands what is happening. Her brother and sister are not asleep and are busy in something not exactly expected from brothers and sisters. Minu knows there is no point reacting to what they are doing however wrong it may be. She comes out to the veranda beside the road. It is actually an open space by the road about two feet wide.

She feels a bit dizzy and nauseated. "It's natural in my condition" thinks Minu. She goes to the tube well nearby, pumps it and puts little water on her head. Splashes some water on her face and feels a bit more relaxed. She starts moving back to her room when suddenly she hears sound of people running in her direction. She quickly hides behind an empty cart left by some vendor who must be living in one of these rooms. She has no watch but she is sure it is late at night, may be one AM or later and people running at this hour can only mean danger. And then she sees them.

Actually it is not a run, it is a chase. A young man called Ritwik is running and he is chased by three men with their faces masked and having chains and daggers in their hands.

Ritwik trips on a stone and cries out in pain as the whole of one of the nails of his right foot has come off. But he can hardly afford to stop and continues the run. The three men, chasing Ritwik curses and continue the chase. For them it is clear it is a fight to the finish today, if there is a fight at all of course. Minu feels that she must do something to save Ritwik, in fact she has saved her once. But before she can think of anything fruitful the party runs past her and a little later the sound of footsteps die away.

Minu gets up from where she was hiding, and starts tottering back to the room when she hears a sharp cry. Surely they have caught Ritwik and have plunged the dagger in his ribs. Murder is not uncommon in these localities. Surely the sharp cry has awakened many a sleeping soul but not a single window opens and nobody tries to peep out. Minu was hoping that somehow Ritwik will get saved; after all he is an intelligent man. Now with the cry all hopes are shattered and Minu falls flat unconscious in front of her door.

* * *

Now we shall go back in time.

This slum in Kumortooli area is a strange world. It's a city within a city with its own norms, own customs and of course own laws. The police seldom enter here and if they enter those are, in most cases, to take away the corpses. The men are either artisans, or some petty vegetable or fish vendors. There are a few houses of women of pleasure who are always in the lookout for fresh recruits.

Flesh trade runs more covertly than overtly though. Many of the girls go out early in the morning for 'work'. While a few really have jobs in various factories around the city and the suburbs most of them work in so called massage parlours, which are veiled forms of brothels. At times costly cars are seen in the vicinity at night when some glad customer offers a lift to the lady after 'work' is over.

Other things running rife in this locality are cheap taverns and gambling. The total turnover in gambling 'trade' is unthinkable for anyone who is not living here or is not associated with the trade by any means. Police gets a good percentage of money in from the gambling houses and in turn they help in covering up the regular brawls that occur in these houses. Only if things go as far as man slaughter they intervene officially.

Though there has been a case when a man, actually a worker of the ruling political party, got murdered in a brawl just outside a gambling joint. The reason was of course allegations of cheating. The police not only changed the case diary to record that the murder had occurred at a totally different place but also gave it a political colour so that the party can gain dividend from the death. Of course for this the gambling joint owner and the political party had to spend quite a sum, but then everything comes with a price.

Ritwik is not a slum dweller. He lives with his elder brother Samir in a two storied house adjoining the slum. Ritwik had lost his parents in a rail accident when he was a school going boy. His elder brother Samir is schizophrenic and at times becomes violent. Ritwik really has a difficult time restraining him. The doctors of the government mental asylum have practically washed off their hands from the case. According to them Samir is incurable. So Ritwik lives a life of constant anxiety about his elder brother. He could have of course handed over Samir to the asylum people, making him a permanent inmate. However he couldn't to do that. He has seen the conditions of the permanent inmates of the so called mental homes. Sub-human would be a very soft and inaccurate adjective to describe their conditions.

The ground floor of Ritwik's house is rented out and is the main source of subsistence for the brothers. Ritwik has a small business though, but the earnings are very modest and also not that regular.

Ritwik is also an ardent party worker.

He had had no interest in politics and saw it as another botheration one has to live with. As only expected from a young man of twenty who is an orphan and living near the slum he was then quite involved with the hooligans running the trade of girls and gambling. Ritwik can still remember that day when he, along with his cronies, sat in a tavern late at night and decided to execute an operation. Abinashbabu was a teacher who lived nearby and was a diehard idealist. He was openly speaking against the illicit liquor trade, gambling and other dark businesses that were the lifelines of the slum. Several times he had written letters to a leading Bengali daily and was also equally vocal about these menaces in the party meetings.

The party had come to power about eleven years back and this was their third term in power. The leaders knew that something is had to be done but were clueless as to how to tackle these problems. After all the support of the entire slum was crucial in winning the municipality as well as the state assembly seat.

Ritwik and his cronies had had warned Abinashbabu several times and asked him to keep his mouth shut. But it was clear by that time that this retired teacher was 'incurable'. So that night when Abinashbabu was returning alone from the party office suddenly he was obstructed by five young men. Without wasting any time in talking they started beating him. In no time he was lying on the ground, covering his face with two hands and kicks were being showered on his whole body. Very soon he had lost consciousness and lay in a pool of blood with one arm and a leg broken.

Ritwik was taking part in the assault but after some time he had refrained. When the team thought that the job of imparting some sense had been done they turned to go. The others went their way and Ritwik was going to his home which was in another direction. When he had walked quite some distance away from the wounded and dying man, he stopped. Even today Ritwik doesn't know what happened to him that moment but he suddenly felt, that what had been done was wrong, gravely wrong.

When Abinashbabu somewhat recovered in the hospital he was interrogated by the police as to what had happened. Ritwik was sure that he had to go to the jail. As Abinashbabu was a respected man and a veteran worker of the party, the party had taken up the case with the police. And it was hardly difficult to understand who could have done so heinous an act. Ritwik's accomplices had already left station as they knew that if Ritwik was identified they would be caught in no time. Ritwik had brought Abinashbabu to the hospital. So attaching him with the crime was no difficult task. And then Ritwik understood that miracles do happen in the world.

Abinashbabu said that he was not beaten up by anyone! It was a hit and run case by an unknown truck. The police officers and the party leaders implored him, threatened him to tell the truth. But he was unshakable.

A few days later Ritwik had an unexpected visitor Abinashbabu!

Abinashbabu did change the life of Ritwik. Since then he is a party worker and a righteous man.

* * *

Ritwik returns home after delivering some goods to his client. It is past mid-day and he has to cook for himself and elder brother. His business is of supplying exercise books and stationary to some schools and small offices. As he cannot afford to keep any helping hand he has to deliver the assignments himself.

It is said that there are six seasons, but the city of Kolkata has basically two seasons. When it is less hot it is summer and for the most of the year it is 'terrible summer'. Carrying loads of books, stationery etc. and going to various offices to deliver is hell of a task. Ritwik feels sad at the thought that after all these he has to cook lunch for himself and his elder brother.

As soon as he enters his own room to change he understands that he had had a visitor. The room has been tidied up, the clothes neatly placed in the wardrobe and the bed has been made with good amount of care. That means Minu had come. That means, in all probability, she has also cooked for Ritwik and Samir. This girl is sort of an enigma. She comes silently when Ritwik is not there and does so many things for him. She is not a great conversationalist. When talked to she answers Ritwik in monosyllables. Many a time Ritwik has told her not to do all these as she has her own business to take care of. But Ritwik knows that he likes these surprises and Minu knows too. And Ritwik knows that she knows.

It had happened a few months after the Abinashbabu incident. Then Ritwik had just started this business of order supply. That night he was returning from a printing press in College Street after delivering an order for paper. Near a particular crossing, and rather a notorious one, he spotted a girl standing alone. She was standing in such a spot where her form was visible but her face was in the shadows. This sight was nothing unusual. Here the girls wait for being picked up. Ritwik could have ignored her and continued his walk but by some strange turn of fate just at that moment a car passed and in the headlights Ritwik could understand that it was Minu. He was surprised as he had never thought that Minu was exactly the call girl sort. Then he looked again. A little observation revealed that Minu was highly uncomfortable. Then he remembered that a few days back he had seen a notorious middle aged lady living in the slum talking with Minu at the corner of the road.

"So this must be her first night" thought Ritwik "something must be done". Ritwik crossed the road and stood in front of her. Minu tried to look away. She knew that Ritwik could not be her 'customer' and was only adding to her ordeal. Ritwik was curt and businesslike.

He simply told her, "This is not your place, come let's go home".

From the core of her heart Minu wanted just that but returning empty handed would mean series of problems. The place where she was standing had come with a price and whether or not she had 'business' she would have to pay. And also returning without money could well mean going without food for the entire night or even more. His debauch of a father had had declared that Minu had to earn her meals. The means of earning mattered nothing to him.

After vacillating for a minute or two Minu decided that she had to listen to Ritwik. She could not accept the life of a whore. Just as she was about to start walking with Ritwik a sedan stopped and a lewd face called out to her with a vulgar whistle. When the man saw that Ritwik and Minu were going away he alighted from the car and obstructed her path. It was a festive night and call girls were scarce. He was not ready to let per prey go so easily. When Minu avoided him and tried to go away he grabbed her arm and started dragging her towards the car speaking filthy language matching his filthy act.

Ritwik could take it no more and as a sharp jab landed on his cheeks the man was thrown off balance and hit the ground. He was of course more hurt than shocked as so long he had regarded Ritwik as a pimp. Ritwik grabbed at the collar of his shirt, pulled up the man and summoned him to leave immediately. The man had rightly sensed that he was no match in strength with Ritwik, cursed and left in his car.

Ritwik did bring Minu home that night and had warned her father of dire consequences if he did dare to misbehave with her. Now Minu does some tailoring work and earns a living. Needless to say that Ritwik did set her up in this trade using his contacts.

Nowadays Ritwik is not quite happy. He had come within the realms of politics inspired by Abinashbabu. Abinashbabu did share with him a lot of inspirational literature. He read the works of Gorki, Tolstoy. Arkady Gaidar and Nikolai Ostrovsky.

Gradually a different world did unfurl itself in front of his eyes. The visuals remained the same, the same old house, the same slum around and the gamblers and the prostitutes. But his interpretation of the world went a sea change. He learnt to respect women, see the sufferings of poor people with utmost compassion. For the first time in his life he was enjoying being among the people and with the people. So far the only thought that that always crossed his mind was how to profit from something or someone. Now he was out of the clutches of endless greed. In the party found quite a few men like Abinashbabu who believed in selfless service. Ritwik was quite fair and handsome and since he was most moved by Gorky's 'Mother' Abinashbabu lovingly called him Pavel after the protagonist of 'Mother'. Those were quite a few years ago.

Now Ritwik finds it hard to relate with various activities of the party and his comrades. The party is in power for many years now and have survived six terms. A steady decline in the level of party workers and the policies is very clear. Also these days, Ritwik feels, the programmes taken by the party are very much mundane and cannot be called 'progressive' by the farthest stretch of imaginative eulogising.

Taverns were always there in the locality but at least they dealt with licensed country liquors. In recent days absolutely illegally made liquor is making way into the market and they are coming in huge quantities. Local tea shops have started selling these hooch at late hours. The consumption is increasing in an exponential rate. A few days back there was a meeting of party workers in the office where curbing this menace was supposed to be the main agenda. The police were cracking down on the traders and the manufacturers and huge quantities of these were being confiscated but now even those raids have slowed down.

In the meeting at first the local leaders made speeches about the menace and how it is affecting the youth. Easy availability always allures the people sitting on the fence. (And in any society of the world these people with questionable allegiance to virtue far outnumber dogmatically righteous souls.) Then a second leader gave some statistics of how much money is rolling into this business and also cited cases where big tragedies have struck as many a times these illegal liquors proved to be deadly poisons.

A growing sense of frustration was gripping Ritwik. After some time he could not take it anymore, stood up and asked, "We are discussing the menace for long with statistics and all that, but what are we doing to curb the menace?" The local leader was going to answer but Sunirmal stopped him. Sunirmal is the state leader who is vying for the ticket for Parliament elections due in a year.

Sunirmal said, "Ritwik you must understand that we cannot take law into our own hands. We are after all a political party and we are not the police. We can assist then police by providing information about the whereabouts and they will take action."

Ritwik had not come unprepared to the meeting. He took out a sheet of paper from his pocket and said, "This paper has the list of all the places in the locality where these liquor pouches are sold and also the names of the principal suppliers."

Sunirmal took the sheet of paper, looked at it for some time and handed it back to Ritwik. "Fine go ahead and report all these to the police" Sunirmal replied," They will take necessary action."

Ritwik smiled and said "I have a friend in the local police station. He was our worker once, now after bagging the job he works for the police."

"Then the job is easy, take his help and lodge a complaint. Some of our other comrades will go with you. That will have more weight. So now comrades can we move to some other important topics?" Sunirmal glanced at his wrist watch. It is customary for big leaders to display that they are always in a hurry.

Ritwik smiled again and said, "My friend in police have helped me. And it is with his help I have compiled the list. They have to keep this list as these are monthly 'collection' points for the police". Silence descended in the room. The local leader gestured Ritwik to shut up and sit down. If the state leader complaints that he was heckled in a local party office by a nobody in presence of the local leader, the local leader will have to face the music. But Ritwik was neither prepared to shut up nor to sit down.

He said, "I want only ten of the party comrades sitting here. If you like you don't call it a party programme. But with these ten men I will shut down this illicit business in two days. My only request is please do not interfere while we carry out the operation."

Sunirmal could feel that the atmosphere of the room was being charged up and he would have to something immediately to douse the fire. He whispered something to the local leader. Then he said, "I am happy to see such spirit with my comrades. I have instructed Suddha (the local leader) to take necessary action. You discuss with him and chart out a programme. So now let us discuss.....” Sunirmal moves to other topics. After the meeting was formally over Ritwik and his close friend Pranab sat with Suddha and asked when they can do the operation.

The leader took his time in lighting a cigarette gave a long drag exhaled and then said, “You must understand the perspective. As a responsible political worker you just cannot jump into an action without understanding the whole story. We cannot indulge in political romanticism like our Maoist friends. While it is true that this hooch trade is a menace we cannot do anything without understanding the whole story. Actually the problem has not originated here nor is limited to our city. It is actually an international problem and has to be tackled accordingly. A sudden impulsive action will only alienate us from the people!”

Abinashbabu is now practically side-lined in the party. These days Ritwik has heard that discussions are on to drop his party membership as he has become too old for party work.

Pranab calls in the afternoon and says something Ritwik was not exactly prepared to hear. Pranab says, “You better be careful Ritwik. I will have to be careful too.”

“But why? Nobody is going to abduct me and ask for a ransom.” Ritwik tries to cut a joke.

“It is much worse than that. Plans are being made to eliminate us or at least teach us a lesson” said Pranab. Ritwik could hardly believe what he heard. Who in the world would have such fantastic idea!

"You do not know Ritwik the power of people associated with this liquor trade. I also had no idea until last evening. It is now an open secret that we are rallying hardest for stopping this trade and so we are now in a vulnerable situation."

"You are trying to make it sound very dramatic" Ritwik again tried to make the conversation light, "Some people may not like us but nobody would dare to touch us. After all we are known as party workers and the party is in absolute power here".

"Forget the party Ritwik" there is now an extra seriousness in Pranab's voice, "if we get hurt or killed the party will simply disown us. Remember that party has refused to take it as official programme."

"But who has told you all these? Is it someone in the party? Tell me the name of the man?" Ritwik is now serious. But he finds that Pranab has already hung up. Ritwik descends into deep thought. He has never discussed the issue except with his party comrades or anywhere outside the confines of the party office. That simply means that the hooch traders have an agent within the party.

Late that night Ritwik receives the news. Pranab is admitted in a hospital after being run over by a loaded truck and is in critical condition. Besides being a party worker Pranab used to run a small tea stall by the side of the road to earn a living. It was closing time and he was alone in the shop.

He was washing some utensils sitting on the side of the road when this truck deliberately ran over him. The matter has been observed by a few men who sleep on the pavement on the other side of the road. Needless to say the miscreant truck has escaped and nobody had the presence of mind or the capability to note the number. As the road was totally deserted at that hour escape was easy.

Ritwik runs to the hospital with a few friends. Pranab has nobody in the world except his father who is old and infirm to a good extent. When Ritwik reaches the emergency ward he finds Pranab's father sitting at a corner and sobbing. The hospital authorities had at first refused to admit Pranab as they said this being a case of accident a case must first be lodged with the police. However, with the intervention of Sunirmal Pranab has been admitted.

When Ritwik reaches him Pranab is already gasping for breath which is clearly terminal breathing. The tires have crushed his legs and part of his abdomen. Ritwik is fighting back his tears. He has something important to do and he does not have much time. He brings his face near Pranab's ear and whispers "Tell me the name Pranab. Is he someone we know? Is he someone within the party?" Pranab has great difficulty in speaking. With his gasping his eyes are bulging out. He still nods his head to say 'yes'.

At that moment Sunirmal enters the room and comes close to the bed. Seeing him Pranab's face changes. In spite of his sorry state a clear look of indignation comes in his eyes and just then his body jerks up twice and then he becomes still. Sunirmal closes his eyes and calls the nurse.

While embracing Pranab's old father in an attempt to console the man who is crying inconsolably Ritwik makes a silent resolution. Party or no party he will continue in his fight.

*   *   *

Kumortuli is famous for making earthen statues of Gods and Goddesses. Every year, around October the city celebrates its biggest festival called Durga Puja or worship of the Goddess Durga. Now the festivities are only one month away and the artisans of Kumortuli are busy making the idols. Minu's father is one such artisan and during this time Minu helps him with the work. Minu knows if she doesn't help her father he would not be able to finish the idol in time and that will result in catastrophe. In this trade like other trades as well reputation means everything. And failure to deliver in time once means shutting off the business for ever. Though he is quite a drunkard Minu's father still manages to bag some orders because he knows his job. All the artisans share a common area or shed made with bamboos and thatched roof for making the idols. The idols have taken shape now. Now they are all in colour of mud and are all naked. The next phase is to paint them and put on the clothing and other accessories. Now the work is slow as the idols need a few days to dry up before paint can be applied. Her father must have gone for booze and Minu is working alone in the shed. She is making the paints ready. The weather is unexpectedly dull and it is raining since morning.

"Cursed luck" thinks Minu. Such weather means the idols will take more time to dry up and be ready for the next phase of work. Because of the weather the shed where she is working is semi dark. The power supply has also failed so she is using a small kerosene lamp. The black smoke of the exposed flame is making the place more shadowy. At this moment she hears voices and footsteps running towards the shed.

After the death of Pranab Ritwik had locked himself up in the house for two whole days. These two days he did devote to chart out a plan for the future. Obviously he has enemies but he cannot afford to sit idle in his home. And then he did start working once again. That day when Ritwik was trying to get information from Pranab in the hospital there was nobody else present in the room for those few minutes. But people did see from outside the room that Pranab was 'talking' with Ritwik.

Surely this had put his enemies ill at ease. Today while returning from an office after delivering the items they had ordered Ritwik senses that he is being followed. Ritwik plans to go towards Strand Bank Road once he hits Bonomali Sarkar Street. It would mean going in the direction opposite to his home in Kumortuli. Going towards the Strand would mean more people and hence he would be safer. But as soon as he hits Bonomali Sarkar Street he understands that way to Strand is blocked as Raghu a notorious miscreant is standing there with two other men. Ritwik starts running towards the East. He has to run towards Kumortuli. The men following him silently so far now start running too uttering words of delight. They know that they are closing in on their prey. Now daggers are glistening in their arms.

A few shops open here and there quickly drop their shutters as they see the chase. Finding no other way Ritwik runs and enters the idol making shed where Minu works with her father.

Ritwik quickly hides behind an idol. But he knows that he is far from safe here. The shed has curtains made from sacks all around but no door that can be closed. Hearing the footsteps Minu comes and finds Ritwik hiding.

"What is the matter?" she asks.
"Shhh..be soft...they are out to kill me Minu"

From the footsteps she has heard Minu knows that Ritwik's assailants have crossed the shed. But they will soon find out and come back. So if something has to be done it has to be done fast. She suddenly sees a bucket with clay kept nearby. This sort of soft clay is used for putting finishing touches to the idols. The traditional idol of Durga shows the Goddess Durga killing the demon and the demon is lying near her feet. Because of regular physical exercises Ritwik has a physique close to the demons as depicted in the idols. She quickly thinks out a plan.

"Please strip...take off all you are wearing" says she. Ritwik is surprised but complies without argument. When he stands stark naked Minu starts applying the soft clay all over his body.

Minu is having a strange feeling. She knows that life of the man she loves is in danger and what she is not a romantic act. But the mystic darkness of the place with so many nude forms around creating an aura of sensuous nature and touching a naked man first time in life are making her excited in a way she has never felt before. She puts layer of clay on his wide chest, his back, buttocks, thighs and his manhood. Ritwik is standing like a statue and though he doesn't like it his body is responding to the touch of a woman. He never knew that such response is possible in a situation when death is looming large. When Minu finishes the job of putting clay she is shivering. She summons Ritwik and asks him to be still in the pose of a demon at the foot of the Goddess Durga in an installation. For some reason this idol was kept incomplete so the demon has not been made. She now brings a mud stained cloth and partially covers Ritwik. Covering the idols being made in such cloth is quite common and now it seemed that Ritwik is only part of the clay idol.

As only anticipated very soon the men chasing Ritwik comes in and demands where she has hidden him. These people are well informed and know that Minu has got a crush for Ritwik.

"I don't know...I am all alone here. You can search if you like" says Minu.

"That we will of course do and if we find him here we will kill you first" says Raghu. A man grabs Minu and makes her sit on the floor and stands guard so that she cannot escape and all others start searching for Ritwik. They are convinced that Ritwik is here and they have to find him.

After searching for nearly half an hour they give up the search. But Raghu is still not sure. He slaps Minu and

demands that she tell the truth once more. She is bleeding from the corner of her lip. She again says, "Why are you beating me? You have searched the whole place...so many of you and you know that I am not hiding him here."
Raghu gives a crooked smile.

"But maybe you are hiding him inside your dress" says he. His friends laugh aloud and before Minu can fathom what is happening Raghu pulls off her dress above her head and another man pulls down her panties and makes her step off them. Now she is standing naked in front of the jeering eyes of lecherous men. She is trying to summon up all the courage that she has, she must not betray Ritwik come what may.

"Ah you are quite a piece! Someday I will show you what it is to be f***** by a real man. And remember if we come to know that you did know where Ritwik is you will be standing like this in the open road." With these words Raghu grabs Minu makes her turn around and kicks her bottom. Minu lands face down on the floor. She doesn't move and stays still as long as she is sure that the miscreants have left.

*   *   *

These days Minu has strange dreams and quite often so. She never knew that such longings were present in her. She longs for Ritwik and wishes to be in his arms. But now even she cannot catch a glimpse of him as Ritwik is outside Kolkata. Just after the incident of ambush his leaders decided that it is extremely dangerous for Ritwik to be here and he must be out of Kolkata for some time. Ritwik has been stationed at a town called Balurghat where he is working under the guidance of the local party leaders.

Little does he know that his leaders in Kolkata are now really worried and are charting out an action plan for the future. Actually they have understood that the party is fast losing ground. A relatively new party born only some eight or nine years back is threatening to dethrone the rulers. Sunirmal is of the opinion a big showdown or a number of big showdowns are necessary to revive the situation. The assembly elections are only nine months away and something is necessary that would yield quick results.

All these days elections were conducted under the surveillance of the state police and it was relatively easier to influence the results. Now because of the insistence of the emerging party the central government has agreed to send central forces making it much more difficult for the state rulers to return to power. One sitting MP has died and bye elections for the single seat is coming up very soon. Nobody knew that the chance of a big showdown will come on that very day of bye elections.

Sunirmal had planned that they would not allow the elections to be peaceful. It has become necessary to prove beyond reasonable doubt that deploying central forces does not help and rather adds to the trouble. A few particular polling booths have been singled out for disruptive operation. One of them is a booth near Apollo hospital. The biggest show of democracy has created many professions hitherto unknown. Sambhu is a professional hooligan who specializes in creating trouble in polling booths and frightens away legitimate voters. His remuneration includes four bottles of country liquor and these have to be provided up front. He drinks two bottles before work and two after. Today also he has become active and has started creating trouble.

The sergeant from Assam rifles has little idea about the realities in Bengal. Also he is quite upset about his duty as his leave has been cancelled. From early morning he has spotted Sambhu as the principal trouble maker and has asked him to vacate the place several times. Instead of listening to him Sambhu is steadily mounting his trouble making activities. At last the Assam Rifles man finds it imperative to use some force and grabs Sambhu by the collar in an effort to physically push him away from the booth. By this time the two bottles of country liquor has set its full effect on him and Sambhu kicks the sergeant and even draws out a dagger. Without waiting for a minute the sergeant unlocks the safety catch of his gun and shoots at Sambhu's feet. A volley of bullets from the automatic rifle leaves Sambhu lying in a pool of blood and crying for his life.

Immediately the situation changes. The voters standing in the queue starts running for their life in all directions. Sunirmal who is nearby rushes to the spot sees the bloody mess and smells fire. Sambhu is very clearly known as close associate of Sunirmal. But Sunirmal is a master in turning an error into account and immediately draws up a plan.

All voters had left the place after the shooting. Sunirmal's boys make the presiding officer and other officials leave immediately. Sunirmal talks with the commander of the

Assam Rifles and says he must withdraw all his men and leave to avoid further trouble. The men from the press are also pushed off a large distance and now the party workers cordon off the place of the shooting where Sambhu is still groaning in pain.

A firing and a wounded is not enough, a death has a bigger impact. If someone dies due to firing of a central force sergeant it will be of big help to stop central forces from intervening in coming elections.

Very soon the news spreads that Sambhu is dead and is a victim of absolutely unprovoked firing by a trigger happy man in uniform.

Police declares curfew in no time to maintain law and order.

*   *   *

The doctor performing autopsy on the corpse receives a note from someone important. The note is short and crisp. The doctor has to pass a verdict of suicide. The doctor utters a bitter curse and orders his assistants to finish the work and stitch up the corpse. After all it's his job and he needs to save it. He cannot disobey the note from the important man. Ritwik has been found hanging in his own room.

A few days after Sambhu's incident Ritwik had come back to Kolkata. Media coverage of the incident had been vast and the spokespersons of various political parties, the political analysts and even some retired police officers who regularly participate in various debates in television had had a hard time running from one TV channel office to another to take part in series of debates aired live.

A huge procession was organized from the party with the corpse of Sambhu. The party news paper and some other dailies who are sympathizers with the party have written heart breaking obituaries about Sambhu. Reading these many people have thought that they had lost a great man and wondered why they didn't know about him before.

Ritwik went straight to the hospital where Sambhu was brought and where he did breathe his last. He also managed to know the specific cause of death as recorded in hospital register. Curiosity has its price and disclosure of knowledge has got a very heavy price.

Sunirmal was not exactly happy to see Ritwik walking in to his office without notice. Ritwik jumped straight to the point.

"I have a few questions about the death of Sambhu" said he. "What else do you need to know? Everything has come in the news" said Sunirmal.
"Sambhu was taken to the hospital at 03PM in the afternoon. The firing did take place little after 12. Why did it take so long to take Sambhu to the hospital?"

Sunirmal tried to look casual and passed his hand casually in his white hair. His hair has greyed prematurely and it does indeed give him a distinguished look.

"How do you know that he was taken to the hospital at three PM?" asks Sunirmal.

Ritwik didn't bother to answer and put his next question which was clearly incriminating for Sunirmal and his followers.

"The register says that the shots were in the legs. When Sambhu was treated it was found that his haemoglobin count was horribly low. He has practically died from excessive bleeding. This proves he was made to lie there and bleed to death. Why did you do it? You have to answer. And now probably you know that everything is not in the news. But I assure you everything will be in the news, soon."

Sunirmal gave a long stare at Ritwik. At last he managed to say, "You can see that I am busy now and so please...It's nothing of the sort what you think. He was killed on the spot by the bullets and there was no delay on our part."

Ritwik stood up.

"What you have done for petty political gains is heinous and you will pay for this" he said before leaving.

He had decided to talk to journalist friend next morning. He didn't know for him there was no 'next morning'.

* * *

Abinashbabu has stopped going to the party office any more. He cannot match their activities with his ideology. Like many others he is also deeply shocked at Ritwik's death. He thinks that Ritwik and suicide just cannot go together.

But that's precisely what has happened. Now Abinashbabu has associated himself with a NGO that mainly provides psychiatric and psychological help to people. This NGO is run by a Christian society.

The other day he was crossing the road when he spotted a mad woman sitting at the corner of the road and talking all to herself. Before being associated with this particular NGO Abinashbabu had had sort of apathy towards men and women who have lost their minds and roaming in the streets. Now he has learnt to look at these people with much more compassion. He has learnt that many of the so called mad men and women we see in the streets are actually curable. He was going past the young lady when suddenly something familiar about the woman struck him. He came near her. The lady is wearing a lose gown and seemed to be pregnant. She had a notebook and a pencil in her hand and was writing something.

Abinashbabu summons the woman to get up and takes her home. The lady, highly careful of the child in her womb moved slowly. The next morning Abinashbabu summoned a cab and took her to the NGO. He cannot let Minu live and die like that in the streets.

The trouble had started after a few days of Ritwik's death. Ritwik was found hanging. Minu suddenly declared that she was pregnant and after much coercing said that she was carrying the child of Ritwik.

After an initial round of thrashing she was dragged to the hospital. The diagnosis made by the doctor left Minu's father spellbound. Not only was she not pregnant, in actuality she was a still a virgin. She had lost her mind. This mental aberration grew every day and at times she also used to have vision of Ritwik running away being chased by men with daggers. After a few days Minu's father and elder brother thought it judicious to dump her in the street corner.

Minu is undergoing treatment now in the NGO. They have provision for few indoor patients. Madhumita, who does the counselling here reports after a few days that Minu is making remarkable progress.

*   *   *

A press conference has been summoned in the NGO. Minu, now fully cured is sitting beside Abinashbabu.

Minu says, "You people have come here as you expect I will tell you something about the incident where Sambhu lost his life. Actually after the shooting I did visit the spot and get this mobile phone. There is a recording in it and in a sense I will say nothing, you will hear everything from Sambhu who is no more."

Minu turns on the sound player in the phone. After some disturbing noises it is heard,

"I am Sambhu...I am dying...I know they will not take me to the hospital...I would have easily lived then...they have cordoned off the area and nobody can come in and save me. If ever anybody finds this recording please, for God's sake tell the people what had actually happened. I can hear they are already chanting slogans in my name calling me a martyr. I am no martyr, nor do I want to be one. I am being murdered. To hell with politics…I…I cannot talk anymore…feeling drowsy…I am no martyr…I want to live… somebody please take care of my child and my wife…"

Surely nobody was paying any attention to Sambhu when he was making this desperate recording.

Minu now lives with Abinashbabu and works in the NGO. After getting cured Madhumita has explained to her that the untold secret was manifesting itself as the unborn child of Ritwik. Minu is happy to be cured and to be able to nurse other patients. She secretly laments though that if only it was not illness. If only she really bore the child of Ritwik.

Then she could feel like the psalms said by the father "Even though I walk through the valley of the shadow of death, I will fear no evil, for you are with me; your rod and your staff, they comfort me."